Big Greasewood

At the end of the Civil War, Reed and Mina Sawyer start a grim search for the small band of rebel bushwhackers who slaughtered their family. As they travel through a bloody Kansas cornfield, across Colorado to New Mexico, fate has other lines of trouble waiting. There's Vernon Claye, the specious owner of Big Greasewood, Cassie Gilkicker and Shelby Hite, the ambitious saloonkeeper. All appear to have a hand in the Sawyers' destiny.

Meanwhile, the bushwhackers under Captain Athol Cade and his wartime cohorts have long since changed their habits, as well as their names and appearances. The end is inevitable, however, and on the night-darkened main street of Las Vegas, a triple-sided shoot out awaits. Reed Sawyer needs help, and he's not primed to lose.

By the same author

Glass Law
The Evil Star
Run Wild
The Black Road
Yellow Dog
Wolf Meat
Cold Guns

Big Greasewood

CALEB RAND

A Black Horse Western

ROBERT HALE · LONDON

© Caleb Rand 2004
First published in Great Britain 2004

ISBN 0 7090 7519 7

Robert Hale Limited
Clerkenwell House
Clerkenwell Green
London EC1R 0HT

The right of Caleb Rand to be identified as
author of this work has been asserted by him
in accordance with the Copyright, Designs and
Patents Act 1988.

Typeset by
Derek Doyle & Associates, Liverpool.
Printed and bound in Great Britain by
Antony Rowe Limited, Wiltshire

1

DEAD FALL

A piercing wind swirled down from Winding Chair Ridge, and Reed Sawyer pulled at a loose button on his chaqueta. Hidden by timber that looked down on the gully below, his mind played with the likely appearance and disposition of the unseen man.

Out front of an old army tent, the embers of a dead fire had been trodden down and some gunny sacks were piled on a wood crate. The man didn't give much away, was no doubt a spare and cautious one. Reed knew that to take him alive, he'd have to go careful. The Sawyers had travelled long and far, were too near now to lose their quarry.

From further up the gully, Reed heard the rhythmic creak of the sluicing cradle, looked to where the sun had westered beyond the ridge. He shifted his gaze to the opposite slope, where the pine afforded good cover for Mina Sawyer. Two hours before, Reed had watched his sister take up position lower in the gully, had seen no movement since.

When they had first arrived, Reed and Mina had quickly picked out the sound of Tripp's diggings. A grubstaker in Manitou had told them that less than a month ago, Tripp had found a gold deposit along a stream off Big Sandy Creek. He was mighty spark-tempered, apparently, was armed at all times, and would shoot a gopher if it ventured too near his claim.

'You two friends o' his?' the grubstaker had asked.

'Yeah, we go way back. He'll just die when he sees us,' had been Reed's sharp reply. Now he smiled grimly. They knew Neavis Tripp all right, though it was only Mina who had actually seen him; just that one time, five years ago. But they both knew a lot about him, how he lived. Reed snorted, was thinking he knew roughly when Tripp was going to die.

The risk of any sound as they crept up on the man was too much, would give them away. With that hair-trigger nerve of his, Tripp would certainly lose control and start shooting. At first dark, they knew he'd quit for the day and return to camp. If they remained in cover, they'd have him between them, could bring him down if he cut up on the other. Reed wanted him alive though, hoped the man would stand steady when he was told to.

The woody squeak of the sluice box ceased then. Reed bit his lip, his already strained senses listening, peering along the gully through the low branches that concealed him.

Shortly, from around a spike of rock in one of the steep banks, Tripp walked into view. Reed sucked air between his teeth, exhaled a quiet oath.

The man had a dark, bearded face around pale eyes. He wore dirt-grimed pants and a ragged linsey-woolsey shirt, a slouch hat pulled low. In one hand he carried a rifle, in the other a fat, hide poke. He walked to the tent and tossed the grain sack through the open flap, rested the rifle barrel across a guy rope. Then he snatched up some tumbleweed to start his supper fire.

Reed moved to ease his cramped muscles, then he rose, hauled in a sharp breath to call his warning.

But Tripp suddenly turned and looked up. He shook himself, yawned, and rubbed at his shoulders. He was facing the slope, for a moment his gaze held to where Reed stood frozen motionless.

Reed hardly dare breathe. He watched anxiously as the man bent to pick up his rifle and a water bucket, as he walked unhurriedly out of sight, back up the gully.

His muscles in tremor, Reed went back into a crouch. Tiny rivers of sweat sliced down his ribs, between his shoulder blades. 'Goddammit,' he grumbled, 'he couldn'ta seen me . . . or could he?

No, he's gone for coffee water, that's all.' But Reed had missed an opportunity and knew it. He should have settled up when Tripp's rifle was on the ground.

Seconds dragged into minutes. Reed couldn't make a move, didn't know how far Tripp had gone beyond the rock spike. Maybe the man *had* seen him. Reed cursed at the thought of Tripp moving around on his position, of Mina being out on her own. He got to his feet, thoroughly scanned the gully, and the silent flanking trees.

Reed stood at six feet, slim, but well muscled. His face carried some small scars, light hair curled down into a short-cut beard that softened the sharp angles of his lower face. His deep, hazel eyes were wide awake and serious.

He started at the crackling of brush. The sound was upslope, perhaps fifty yards to his rear, and he checked himself from calling out to Mina. It won't be a woodland critter with us around, he thought. Tripp's seen me, thinks I'm here to filch his poke.

He ain't leavin' his precious dust behind. He's workin' his way behind me to get a safe, close shot.

Reed listened for another revealing sound. When he heard the light crack of a snapping twig, he left his cover. He went up the steep incline fast through the soft needles, leaves and blowdown. As he dodged the crowded timber, he hoped that Mina would stay hidden till he knew what was going on.

He caught a glimpse of Tripp, head lowered as he came downslope. Reed pressed himself against the thick trunk of a pine, hardly revealing his face as Tripp worked his way closer. Then the man saw him and halted in his tracks.

Reed was ready for him, wasn't going to wait for a better or healthier time.

'Drop your gun, Tripp,' he shouted. He was going to say he wasn't interested in the gold, decided it didn't matter.

Tripp wasn't caught completely unaware, and he uttered a sharp, reckless gasp, as he brought up his rifle. Its roar sent wild echoes around the trees and rocks and the bullet smashed bark from the pine a few feet above Reed's head. Tripp swung away up the slope with Reed lunging after him, crashing pell-mell through the timber.

The slope sheered up to where trees and brushwood thinned at the timberline. Tripp was just ahead now, scrambling on the shale escarpment, leaping from the shelter of outcrops to escape the compass of Reed's rifle. Then the man lost his balance in the loose rock. He made a grab at the root of a gnarled jackpine, gained a foothold, but lost his rifle. It clattered down the rock face, to land near Reed's feet as he broke from timber.

Reed stopped running and looked up into the gloomy light. He saw Tripp clinging to the wind-blasted tree, and found an icy smile.

'That's as far as you go, Tripp. Now I come and get you,' he rasped.

In response, Tripp shoved a trembling hand at the butt of his Colt. Reed shook his head once, hissed disapproval as he swung up his rifle and levelled the foresight. He squeezed off a shot as Tripp drew his gun. Tripp yelled and, holding his shattered arm, rolled in at the base of the tree. He went into an agonized, frightened silence as Reed immediately made his way up the escarpment.

But the prospector saw that Reed's intention was to get above him. He let out a long groan and moved, scrambled higher.

The fearful drive of his legs shook down a small landslide, and Reed continued to curse violently. But his climb was now single-minded as he made his way toward the higher rimrock.

Reed heard Tripp's moaning as he closed the distance between them. Tripp pulled himself on to a narrow ledge, his grey, pain-filled face peering over its brink. He kicked out at a pile of split rock, and Reed shrank helplessly against the cliff face as the chunks of shale came crashing down around him.

Reed coughed and choked as dust and rock dirt showered over him. Ramming the flat of one hand into a fissure he leaned out. He saw there was a foothold to his left and he swung his body sidelong, away from directly under Tripp's ledge.

Having left his rifle below, Reed drew his own Colt and fired two bullets into the rimrock above. The rotten stone burst apart like grapeshot, and from kicking down more rock, Tripp squeezed himself back from the edge.

With hot breath rasping in his throat, Reed resumed his climb towards the defenceless Tripp. Within a few minutes, he'd reached a point level with the ledge, then he worked his way towards it.

Tripp shrivelled into his tight spot, and holding his useless arm, he watched Reed climb inescapably closer. Then his head fell forward, and through the hazy eyes of pain, he stared at the ground between the scuffed leather of his boots.

Reed caught him by collar of his tight black coat and, with one angry, determined effort, dragged the man to his feet.

'Take the gold, it's . . .' Tripp began.

'I don't want your gold. Just look at me,' Reed yelled into the man's face.

Tripp blinked at the choking grip, the overall pain. 'What? I never seen you before . . . don't know you,' he scraped out uncertainly.

'You've seen the likeness,' Reed almost spat the words. 'There was a man an' his wife, an' a girl no more'n a kid. They were on a farm just outside o' Lawrence, Kansas. Think back a few years, Tripp, to the time o' Bloody Bill Anderson. You had quite an army in '63. But most of 'em are dead now.'

Seeing the terror drag at Neavis Tripp's eyes, Reed paused for effect.

'There musta been a lot o' burned-out cornfields you an' them Bushwhackers rode away from, eh?' he persisted threateningly. 'My name's Reed Sawyer, an' some o' those people you butchered were Sawyers, too. They were most o' my family.' Reed ground his teeth, and without anything more, he lifted his arm, flung the man hard against the cliff wall. Tripp dropped to his hands and knees. His gimlet eyes blinking through the hair that fell long and greasy from his head.

'You followed me all the way from there ... all these years?' he questioned fearfully.

'Yeah, but there's two of us, an' we got the names of all you murderin' scum,' Reed said dully. 'Anderson got the back of his head shot away, an' two more were shot down by the Feds. That left three. You, and a lieutenant named Dawse Packman, and Captain Athol Cade. The three of you ran west into Colorado, went your separate ways.' Reed moved in close, his fists were clenched, his knuckles white. 'Where are they, Tripp?' he rasped. 'Where's Cade an' Packman, goddamn you?'

'What happens if I tell you?' Tripp asked.

Reed leaned down and caught him by the throat, shook him, then pressed real hard with his thumbs.

'I've lost the blood lust, you gutless slime, not my memory. You're goin' to die one way or another.' Reed let off the squeeze, let Tripp suck in some wind.

'New Mexico. Both of 'em gone to Las Vegas,' the man croaked. 'You goin' to kill me now?' he asked in despair.

Reed let him go, breathed heavy while he considered it. Not fair, he thought, how the beginning and the end could happen almost within the same moment. After five years, there was suddenly no savour. The hunger for killing Tripp wasn't as sharp as that for a slice of pie.

Reed was backed up to the rimrock, and he half turned to glance down at the voice that hailed from below. It was Mina, at the base of the cliff. She was looking up, her face taut with concern. Reed waved at her reassuringly. He didn't understand soon enough his sister's pointing, her next shout of warning, and he was too late. Mina had seen the sudden shifting movement of Tripp on the ledge.

The man scrambled to his knees and, in desperation, rammed the heel of his hand against Reed's chest. There was little strength behind the shove, but with the narrow rimrock at his heels there was no stepping back. For a moment, Reed teetered wildly, tried to counterbalance forward, twist his weight sideways. But it wasn't enough, and he flailed into the drop.

He grabbed at the rotted shale as he fell, caught his weight with a shock that almost disjointed his fingers. The rock crumbled, but he took hold, hung straight-armed. He clung on, his upper body hugging the rough rock. His legs were stretching, digging for a foothold, but they found none. Then he flung back his head and saw the man above raise a boot, knew what was coming.

Before Tripp's heel crunched down on to Reed's fingers, Mina's rifle made a sharp, ear-splitting report. Its echo crashed around Reed's head, carried on, as Tripp's gulping cheer died.

Neavis Tripp turned slowly in mid stride, and foamy specks of bright blood touched Reed's face as the man pitched out over the rim. 'Go get your goddamn gold,' Reed whispered hoarsely, as the body fell past him fifty feet to the floor of the gully.

Mina glanced briefly at Tripp's bloody, shattered body, then she lowered her rifle. 'I'm comin', big brother,' she shouted up. 'Don't you go droppin' off, just yet.'

Craning his head, Reed looked down. 'You got a couple o' minutes, sis. For Chris'sakes no longer,' he gasped.

From below and out to his left, Reed heard Mina began to climb. How long's she goin' to take? Which bones break first? Reed wondered morbidly as the dragging pain shot from his fingers to his arms and into his shoulder sockets. He turned the side of his face against the rock face, squeezed his eyes shut. He recalled a story told about the scout, Jim Bridger. It was said he'd kept a supply of birch twigs in his pockets, used them as splints for the fingers he snapped when climbing through the Rockies. Up till now, Reed had always thought of that as a tall tale.

Then silver stars began to explode in the blackness behind his eyelids as his fingers eased their grip. He cursed his luck, was hoping the end would be quick, when he felt Mina's hands grip tight and fast around his wrists.

He strained his neck backward, stared into the

welcome and smiling face of his sister.

'I got you. Get yourself a footin' when I pull,' Mina said, and with her heels set, she heaved backward.

Reed felt his body rack at the joints, but he stretched out, hooked his toes into a fissure in the sloping underside of the ledge. 'I got a hold,' he gasped. 'But you ain't strong enough. I'm goin' to fall.'

'Yes I am, an' no you're not,' Mina told him, and her hand closed around Reed's left arm above his elbow. She pulled, and Reed moved up, got a grab at the rock with his right hand.

'All you got to do is climb. Now!' Mina shouted, and hauled back as Reed kicked his feet at the rimrock.

A few moments later, and desperately gulping air, Reed scrambled over and on to the ledge, wrapped himself around Mina's boots.

'Where'd you get to be that tough?' he said, as Mina helped him to his feet.

Mina rubbed her arms and shoulders. 'Milkin' the cows, grapplin' hogs an' pullin' corn, I guess,' she said with a thankful smile. 'I'm hopin' he told you somethin', Reed. I'm hopin' *real* bad.'

'He did. Mina. They're in Las Vegas.' Reed replied, then spat some dust over the ledge.

'*They*? Who's *they*, exactly?'

'Cade an' Packman. They rode there together.'

The Sawyers stood looking thoughtfully at each other. They'd ridden many a mile over the years, always with the same intent, the same single purpose. And now they had a lead on where it would end.

It was Mina who voiced her concern.

'If someone was goin' to kill me, I reckon I'd lie for the spite. Las Vegas must be more than two hundred miles. What do you reckon we should do?'

'Head south,' Reed said, with a droll edge. 'But first, we got to get the hell off this mountain.'

2

DARK CAMP

Reed and Mina had taken care of Neavis Tripp. They were short on ceremony, just rolled him in his tent with his traps and gunny sacks.

Now, a short week later, Mina whistled softly as they skirted the Turkey Mountains, rode the west bank of the Canadian. They were well into New Mexico, many miles south of Raton, and hoping to make Las Vegas by nightfall.

'You still carry that little wood-carved thing?' Reed asked.

Mina's hand dipped inside her coat, pulled out an Apache love doll that had worn smooth and polished over the years. 'Sure do,' she said, smiling. 'Never been anywhere without her.'

Still holding the effigy, Mina nodded to the east, where low-banked clouds scudded down from the Sangre de Cristos. 'Goin' to be one big soakin', when that hits us,' she said. 'We got about an hour to find some shelter.'

'I reckon we'll push on. At least get close, before full dark.' Reed responded with little consideration, and Mina understood.

Reed thought that riding into Las Vegas was a bit like getting stung to find out if the scorpion's sting would kill you or not. So strange, that after a five-year quest, he was bothered at maybe a few hours' delay.

The grey raincloud mingled fast with early dusk. Behind the riders, a covey of bobwhites flushed from the mountain slopes wheeled down into the scrub. Then the storm rolled in, and they felt the first buffets of a big wind. With heads bent under the torrential downpour, Reed and Mina hugged the course of the creek looking for a sheltering outcrop in the bank. Then, a hundred yards ahead, they saw a stand of cottonwood and rode towards it.

They weren't the only ones who'd had the same idea though, and it wasn't long before they caught the ruddy glow of a fire ahead of them. Neither of them said a word, nor hauled in. They both knew they weren't going to find friends in that territory, but who would turn anyone away on such a night? Reed threw a glance at Mina, saw her mouthing suitable imprecations. He saw her pull aside her sodden duster and palm the butt of her Colt.

Nearing the fire, Reed saw it was situated tight beneath the overhang of the dripping trees. A man stepped to the rim of hazy firelight and peered through the dimness. His call was razor sharp, carried a nervy warning.

'Name yourself, pilgrim.'

'Friends. Two of us,' Reed answered.

'Then come in, straight an' slow.'

Reed heeled his roan into the dim glow, swung down and gently dropped the reins.

The man was outlined against the fire and his face was in shadow. 'Warm your hands,' he said, looking into the darkness beyond Reed.

Walking stiffly to the fire, Reed glanced and nodded to another man who was sitting with his back to a tree. He sat on his heels, and spread his chill fingers at the meagre warmth.

'You said there was two o' you. Where's your company?' the first man asked suspiciously.

Holding the reins of her own horse, and as if on cue, Mina stepped forward.

The man looked hard at her. 'Do I know you from somewhere?' he tested, as the light touched at Mina's face.

Mina gave a thin smile. 'I hope not,' she replied, moving towards Reed and the fire. The man sniffed, hemmed and hawed, sniffed again. 'Nights like this, ain't for decent folk,' he said, and took a couple of steps to the side.

Reed saw the man's hair was very dark, and his face was lean. His features were small and pinched to go with his manner. Reed also noticed the holster, belted tight around the outside of his slicker. No, not a night for decent folk, Reed concurred.

The other man rose to his feet with the ease of youth. Reed met his challenging stare with unblinking calm. The youngster was of sturdy build: he wore dust-caked range clothes, and his broad, open face was topped by fair curly hair. Reed guessed a trace of wildness was holding him just short of maturity.

'We'll try to stay obligin',' Reed said calmly.

His words seemed to disappoint the boy who glanced at Mina, then at the dark man, who smiled coldly and shrugged.

Mina broke the hung silence. 'Well, I'll just unsaddle these mounts, Reed, maybe find some stuff for the fire.'

The boy relaxed and laughed. 'Got yourself a bondswoman, eh mister?' he asked Reed. 'Goin' to get me one, one day.'

Mina had swung her left hand up to the horn of Reed's saddle. She glanced easily at the boy, her voice gently teasing. 'It's a good idea. She'll be able to fork your peas . . . wash your diapers.'

The dark man sniggered, while a stifled cough came from the kid's throat. His hand moved, and his fingers touched the holster of his sidearm. He didn't move any more though, because Mina already had her own Colt aimed at the middle of his face. Quickly, Reed stepped closer to the dark man. He'd seen the same situation before, and it never ceased to amaze him. It was the look on a man's face – usually an advancing one – at Mina's capability with a gun. He also knew how Mina would handle it. To her, the bettering was enough, generally won the day.

The dark man took on the clash with the shrewdness of age. 'That's the way we learn, Caw. Expect the unexpected,' he said knowingly.

The boy remained very still, then a smile almost shaded his face as he got back down to his blankets.

He's not put out much, Reed thought, just got some horse sense. And he liked him, in the same perverse way that he disliked the dark man.

Mina dragged their saddles near to the fire. She tied-in the horses to a ground rope then went out again into the darkness. Reed stood by the fire and pulled off his saturated jacket. Then he drew out his sougan and spread his ground tarp. He wrapped himself in the blankets and settled where he could watch both men.

It was the dark-faced one who walked over to him.

'Don't normally not know who I'm sharin' camp with,' he said. 'The name's Herran Tudor, out o' West Texas. The kid's Cawden Fisher. Says he's out o' Doc Holiday an' Big Nose Kate.'

Reed raise an eyebrow, thought for a second then chuckled. 'Reed Sawyer,' he said.

Tudor's dark brows tightened. Thoughtfully, he squatted down and picked up a handful of dirt, worked it between his fingers. 'Where'd you two meet up?' he asked, meaning Mina.

'Lawrence, Kansas. Our ma introduced us.'

'Your ma?' Tudor questioned.

'Yeah. She's my sister,' Reed said, and saw some

irritation bite at the dark man. He'd heard of Herran Tudor. A border *gringo*, someone associated with trouble and shady deals, nothing to pin down. But they were frontier tales and lost nothing in the telling, he thought wryly.

As for Cawden Fisher, there was something about him, and Reed sensed that he hadn't yet gone bad. But he was travelling in bad company. Company that would most likely run him to a forking of the road.

Mina returned with her arms wrapped around some dry duff. She tossed a couple of handfuls on the fire, then some not-so-dry branch wood. The duff ignited like a swarm of fireflies, the wood crackled and the flames flared higher.

'Hang your duster, Mina. Get it dried out for the mornin',' Reed said.

'Yep, make yourself right at home, why don't you,' Fisher, added cheekily. The youngster stood up, drew his pistol from its holster and spun the cylinder. He looked around, away from Reed, Mina and Tudor, saw an empty milk can lying in the outreach of the firelight. He brought the gun up, took aim and fired. One of the horses snorted its displeasure, as the can skittered six feet across the bare ground. The kid smiled and aimed again as a second bullet jumped the can and a gob of dirt into the darkness. But it wasn't him who fired the second shot, and his defiant stare swung around to Tudor.

Tudor was laughing to himself as he sheathed his gun. 'Always finish what you start, Caw.

Suppose that was a big gunny Sawyer . . . not a little ol' tin can?'

'Funny dumbsters,' Reed muttered and closed his eyes. He opened them five minutes later, when Mina jogged his elbow. His sister handed over cold fry bread and salt pork rashers from their saddle pouches. Reed chewed slowly, washed it down with swallows from his canteen. After a leisurely smoke, he reached for his gunbelt and unholstered his gun. Like Mina's, it was a hickory-gripped Navy Colt, its barrel reamed and cylinder converted to take brass cartridges. The matched guns were going to be Reed's coming-of-age gift from his father. But things turned out different. They collected one each, and early.

Tudor and Fisher watched hopefully, but seeing him start to clean the blued steel, Tudor smiled thinly and the kid snorted his disappointment.

Mina stretched out in her blankets, kept her eyes half open till Reed gave her a nod. She breathed with satisfaction, closed her eyes and almost immediately claimed sleep. Reed smiled faintly, wished he had a big brother to protect *him*. He thought back to their early, inseparable days. As far back as his memory reached, he'd looked out for Mina. He'd brought to bear his two years' seniority and toughness, although reality maybe had it otherwise.

The sleep-induced images were less clear nowadays. But the facts stayed the same. They'd never change.

*

It had been three full years after Reed Sawyer had marched off to war before he returned to his family's farm. He was ten miles from home, when he'd had to evade a group of rebel guerrillas. Sweaty and bloodied, they'd ridden past him fast, heading east along the turnpike. For some ill-fated reason, Reed thought he should remember their faces, and he looked hard at the two who rode a short distance behind.

It had been the forewarning, and Reed found the family house and buildings reduced to wood ash. The bodies of his ma and pa were laying in the charred cornfields where they'd been beaten and shot dead. Mina was face down in a trailside ditch where she'd crawled with a cracked head and a sabre slash in her side.

Later, through a breaking fever, Mina had whispered the story. A group of raggedy, wild-looking soldiers had ridden in. They'd demanded money, anything of value. War booty, their father had said. The men had called him a Jayhawker, then shot him and their mother where they'd stood, working in the fields. They'd found the two girls, dragged them from the fraidy hole where Pa had told them to hide. Mina recalled nothing more, except lunging at one of the men, who wore a hat with a red cockade. She struggled with him for his carbine, then there was the flash of steel, the hot searing pain.

Reed tended to Mina's wound. He made her comfortable with some salvaged food and water, before riding back in the direction of Topeka. He came to a neighbouring hog farm, a few miles along the turnpike, where the farmer told him the heartbreaking news. The man had been out feeding his stock, when he'd found the girl's body. It was on a low-rising mound, near to where some men had evidently cold-camped before moving on.

Reed had borrowed a wagon to bring his youngest sister's body home, and the following day, he laid her to rest alongside his parents.

'We ain't stayin', are we, Reed?' Mina had asked, her face damp, still smudged with dirt.

'What d'you reckon?' Reed said determinedly, looking east towards the turnpike.

That, as Reed now reflected, wasn't much more than either of them had spoken about their dogged undertaking. Reed was for taking Mina east, to distant relatives in Louisville, Kentucky. But she said no, undertook to pull her weight. Reed saw the determination, knew she was owed the retribution.

Once away from Lawrence, Athol Cade and his bushwhack riders had left a trail of bloody carnage as they headed west. General Ewing of the Union Army immediately ordered the Missouri border counties to be scoured, to find and bring to justice the rebel outlaws.

With the consequent and, almost immediate deaths of Bill Anderson and a few others, it seemed that Reed and Mina had undertaken the briefest of missions. So they turned back east, into dead ends and cold trails, in what seemed an useless pursuit from the Smoky Hills in Kansas, to the Rockies in Colorado. Their reason for staying west was that the men they sought would be well away from both Ewing's wrathful command and Kansas lawmen. In long, ensuing years they combed the vast territory between the South Platte and Arkansas rivers, asked questions without number, searched untold faces.

Then at last, while talking to a man in the mining town of Manitou, the name of Neavis Tripp was mentioned, and their search neared its end. The word came from the old grubstaker who'd sold Tripp a lamp and some tools. Reed bought drinks then, roostered with him good and proper.

And now Tripp was dead. But only after bequeathing the fact that Athol Cade and Dawse Packman were in Las Vegas.

Reed stared at the rain that fell incessantly from the leaves of the cottonwoods. Had Cade and Packman had a change of identity? It would be likely enough, considering the nature and scope of their crimes. They could be anything from bankers to dollar-a-day ranchhands.

Reed looked at Tudor who was hunkering a few feet away. The man's eyes were blinking against a thin trail of smoke that drifted up from a cigarette.

'If you people are still headed for Las Vegas, we'll ride along. If that's OK?' Tudor said.

'We're still headed there. Yeah, I guess it'll be OK,' Reed said drily.

'Good. You lookin' for work, you an' your sister?'

'Not necessarily. Why? You offerin'?' Reed asked.

Tudor stretched out to grind his heel into the butt of his cigarette. 'I got to see a man. He might have somethin' for the right person. I could put in a word,' he added casually. Then he walked slowly across to his saddle sack and bedroll, near to Cawden Fisher, who was already into light snoring.

Reed remained sitting with his chin on his knees. His cleaned and loaded gun was in his fist beneath his blanket. He looked into the deep dark, didn't want the night blindness that came from firegazing. His life might depend on it. Despite his exhaustion he decided to stay awake, was asleep within two minutes.

3

WORKING GUN

With Herran Tudor and Cawden Fisher riding ahead, Reed and Mina trailed into the main street of Las Vegas. The still rising sun picked out a few stately old adobes whose Spanish adornment contrasted with the clapboarded frames of more recent construction. Along the rutted street, the night's rain stood in pools, oozed thick and heavy around the hoofs of their horses.

Tudor drew up at a false-fronted building that carried a red-painted HITE'S SALOON sign across its entrance. He dismounted, draped his reins around the hitch and looked up at Reed.

'You'll be takin' a drink? A dirt cutter, at least?' Tudor asked.

Mina nodded her support for the idea, reached over to take Reed's reins. 'I ain't goin' anywhere,' she said.

'No don't. I won't be more'n a minute,' Reed answered.

As they went inside, Tudor shot Reed a curious glance 'That sister o' yours got some problem?' he asked.

'It ain't really a problem. She just don't drink if she thinks she's goin' to shoot somebody,' Reed replied flatly, his eyes quartering the saloon.

The room was long and low-ceilinged. But there was no rich odour, no heavy pall of smoke. This early in the morning, the bar was clear of customers. Reed asked for a beer, Tudor and Fisher took whiskey.

'To wine an' wild women,' Tudor said, swallowing his drink in one go. 'I'm Herran Tudor,' he said to the barkeep. 'The boss'll be expectin' me.'

The man stopped adjusting his stem-winder. He glanced at Reed and Fisher, ran his eyes carefully over Tudor. He considered something for a moment, then nodded toward a rear door. 'The office is back there.'

Tudor snapped a silver dollar on the bar top. 'Stay around, why don't you. Meet the boss. He might have some work,' he said, looking at Reed.

'You're forgettin' there's two of us, an' it ain't work we came here lookin' for. I'll be thankin' you for the drink . . . sayin' good day.'

Tudor shrugged, walked to the office door and went straight in uninvited.

Reed considered the sticky froth on the side of his glass, wished Cawden Fisher hadn't been there. He had one or two things to enquire of the barkeep. He sucked at the lees of his beer and turned away from the bar. He acknowledged Fisher, took a step towards the door when Tudor called out.

'Heh, Sawyer. Hold up an' meet someone.'

A man stepped around Tudor, came across the room. He was very tall, had a long, wispy beard which ran neatly down the front of his pleated shirt. His eyes were chilly, black beads.

'This is Shelby Hite,' Tudor said keenly.

Hite extended a bony-fingered hand. 'Mr Sawyer. Herran tells me you're seeking employment,' he said, in a clipped, southern drawl.

The saloon owner carried himself with a confident, martial bearing. For Reed, it wasn't a propitious start, made him more unsettled than he was already.

Hite held up his hand for the barkeep's attention. 'The bourbon. And three glasses, if you please, Chase.'

'Four,' Tudor corrected. 'Cawden Fisher here's with me.'

Hite settled his piercing countenance on young Fisher. 'Why, he's no more than a shave-tail, Herran. Besides, you'll be handling this job alone.'

Fisher levelled his own stare at Hite. 'In a *real* army, shave-tails get to be promoted,' he retorted.

'They sure do, boy,' Hite said, his face cracking thinly. 'Well if it's a field promotion you're after. . . ? Pour him a drink, Chase.'

Reed took a sip of the fiery-smooth liquor, wondered about young Fisher's use of 'army', assumed it was something he'd picked up from Tudor.

'Mr Sawyer. I have a problem,' Hite started off without preliminary. 'I've got some men, but they're not up to much . . . mostly from mongrel outfits. I need more proficient help for Mr Tudor.'

He's got a problem all right, Reed thought. Like Tudor, he's thinking I'm a hired gun, looking for work. That part of the south-west was almost ignored by officials in the county seat. Federal lawmen had very little occasion to visit. It was men like Hite who held power, played put-and-take with their own notion of justice.

'Supposin' me an' my sister accept your offer: exactly what sort o' help we expected to provide?' Reed asked, without any obvious committal.

Hite almost laughed. 'Until I decide otherwise, Mr Sawyer, the specific nature will remain the business of the paymaster. Now, how would you think on. . . .'

The sound of a slapping harness drew Hite's attention away from Reed. He walked quickly to the half door that led into the street. He turned around, indicated that Tudor come and take a look.

'That's him. That's Colonel Claye,' Hite said, then lowered his voice, spoke in an eager whisper. Tudor asked a question or two, listened and nodded. Then he pushed open the door and stepped on to the porch.

Reed and Fisher walked over to the door. Looking downstreet, Reed saw a red-haired girl stepping down from an open-topped buggy. She was taking the hand of an elderly man who was dressed in a frock-coated white suit.

'Who're they?' Reed asked.

'Vernon Claye. He owns Big Greasewood ... biggest spread this side of Santa Fe. The girl's his daughter, Mercy.'

'If *he's* your problem, he sure don't look like much o' one from here.'

'He's going to look even less like one after Herran's done,' Hite said sharply.

'What the hell's he goin' to do to an old man in broad daylight?'

Hite almost spat his response. 'He's going to have the *advantage*, that's *what*. Without his men, Claye will need a lot more than his Godfearing pride.'

Reed watched with disturbed interest as Vernon Claye stooped to check his rig mare's forehoof. The man was slight, almost frail, but his features appeared to be set firm.

'At last, I'll get to see some fear in the old buzzard's face,' Hite said.

'You'll see it in more'n his,' Reed snapped, and brushed past. He went through the saloon door just as Tudor started his walk across to the buggy. Behind him, he heard the raw disbelief in Cawden Fisher's voice.

'You sent Herran out there to hurt that old man?'

'Sure takes a while for you to get bit, don't it, boy,' Hite mocked. 'You must know what Tudor is, you came in with him.'

'We never talked about nothin' like that,' Fisher replied with a shaky voice. 'Christ, Mr Hite, that girl's right there, she . . . she. . . .'

The boy was just about reaching his fork in the road, but Reed couldn't wait for him to make up his mind. As he stepped down from the sidewalk, Hite's voice cleaved the air.

'Stay out of this, Sawyer. You've nailed your colours.'

'Not yet, I haven't. There was a time when I couldn't do much about this sort o' thing: now I can,' Reed said quietly.

Hite sucked in an enraged breath, but before he could do or say anything, Cawden Fisher pulled his Colt. He calmly cocked the hammer, and shoved it deep into Hite's side.

'Let him be, mister. This is watchin' fun. No interferin',' he threatened.

Off the corner of the saloon, Reed gave Mina a 'don't get involved' shake of his head, then started to cross the street.

Tudor was standing no more than a dozen paces from the old man. 'You there,' he shouted, offensively.

Vernon Claye lowered the horse's hoof, looked slowly around him. 'Are you talking to me or the mare?' he asked calmly, when he saw Tudor staring him down.

'I'm talkin' to you, goddammit. Not that there's much difference between your face an' the horse's arse.'

With a slightly trembling hand, Claye brushed back a flap of his suit, showed a polished cavalryman's holster. 'I don't know you, sir, or why you're provoking me. Perhaps you're drunk and mistaken. Just apologize to my daughter for your foul mouth, and we'll forget it. You can move on.'

'Well, ain't you the speechifier,' Tudor sneered. 'Ain't you goin' to duel me with that ol' fightin' piece you're carryin'?'

'Pa, don't,' the girl shouted. 'It's what he wants. He's a Hite gunman.'

'Get out of the way, Mercy. Do as I say, girl,' Claye answered.

Then, from the middle of the street, Reed's voice joined in. 'Tudor, leave the ol' feller be,' he called.

'Hah, Sawyer,' Tudor said, but didn't turn. 'I had a gut feelin' about us. But now, I'm right busy, so it'll have to be another time.'

'The time's *now*, Tudor. I'll shoot your legs from under you if you pull a gun on the oldster,' Reed said impassively.

Tudor took a step back, then made a half turn, stood sideways on to Reed. His small, dark features were pinched with menace.

'In situations like this, you know the mistakes most men make?' he asked.

'Yeah, they talk too much,' Reed replied, as an evil-grinning Tudor went for his gun. The two gun blasts merged into one, reverberated between the buildings along the street. Reed had made a small movement, and Tudor's bullet thumped the top of his left shoulder, inches from his neck. But a great hammer blow caught Tudor. Reed's bullet entered his chest beneath his outstretched gun arm and he fell immediately. There was no other sound, just the mud water slurping at his body as he hit the street.

Reed lowered the barrel of his Colt as he walked over to Tudor's body. 'Nobody's *that* busy,' he muttered. He didn't want to look up, felt a churning sickness in his stomach. He put a hand to his sweating face and looked at Vernon Claye.

The old man's look was stern and unmoving. 'I didn't ask for your help,' he said, 'whoever you are.'

'Reed Sawyer, and I know you didn't. But I had my reasons. At least you're alive to chew someone out.'

Claye was dabbing at his face with a big handkerchief. 'That I am, sir,' he said. 'But unfortunately you've tied me into a debt.'

Reed shrugged. 'Well, like I said, I had my reasons, an' it's not a debt I'm likely to hold you to.'

'But we are indebted, Mr Sawyer.' Mercy Claye moved close to her father. She was tall and slim. Not pretty, but she had her father's handsome looks, and Reed liked it. 'Me, most of all,' she added.

'Then I'll remember *that*,' Reed said, finding a seldom-used smile. Then he nodded and touched the brim of his hat.

With a face adjusted to iron-hardness, he walked

back across the street.

At the saloon hitch, Mina was sitting with their horses. She gave a curt nod. '*Some minute,*' she said.

Shelby Hite was standing inside the doorway. 'You've had your fun, cowboy,' he rasped, 'but now you ride on. Cross me again, and it'll be the last.'

Reed didn't say anything. But he felt the sickness rise again, the upshot of hostility twisting his vitals.

Cawden Fisher eased his Colt back into its holster as Hite gave him a long, calculating look.

'You pulled a gun on me, boy. I suggest you eat the Sawyers' dust,' the man advised.

Fisher sniffed and shook his head slowly. 'No, I don't think so,' he said. Then he pushed through the door and went straight to his horse. He nodded at Mina, heeled into a fast canter down the centre of the street.

Hite went to the bar and poured himself two good fingers of the bourbon. Then he bit the end off a long, thin cigarillo and spat it towards Reed. Without another word or a backwards glance, he strode to his office.

4

THE GILKICKER CLAIM

Outside of Hite's Saloon, Reed stepped down to the street. He took the reins of his roan from Mina.

'We'll take the horses up to the livery stable. Find us a hotel, maybe.'

'You've been told to ride on. I heard,' Mina reminded her brother.

'I'm not takin' his goddamn orders, Sis. You forgettin' why we're here? Anyways, Hite ain't a lawman, and I ain't in the army no longer ... his or anyone else's.'

The Sawyers heeled their horses toward the livery barn at the north end of town. Reed felt a small satisfaction at Cawden Fisher's response to the conflict. Likely they'd not see him again, but it confirmed Reed's estimation, and the kid was out of Tudor's influence. Furthermore, Reed had helped Vernon Claye. But in doing it without considering the whys and wherefores, he'd created a powerful adversary in Shelby Hite. Yep, a good day's work, so far, Reed thought wryly.

Reed and Mina were walking their horses alongside the hardware store. Reed glanced at the girl who was standing under the canvas awning.

'Excuse me. Could I have a word, please?' she said.

Reed turned the roan's head. 'You talkin' to me, ma'am?' he asked.

'Yes. I saw what happened. I'd like to talk to you.'

Reed looked at Mina, thought for a moment before responding. 'What about?' he asked. 'You a sheriff? A reporter, maybe, ma'am?'

'No. But I've seen men shoot each other dead before. Even saw a woman do it once.'

Reed looked at Mina again, who shrugged, but managed to look curiously interested.

The girl had dark eyes and dark hair, and she wore an outfit that didn't lean towards any recent toil.

'I'm Catherine Gilkicker,' she continued. 'If you can afford me a few minutes, I've got a proposal that could be to your advantage ... both our advantages. Please? Ten minutes?'

'Mina, you take the horses on to the stable,' Reed decided.

'Yes, boss. Will there be anything else, boss?' Mina said, her eyes flashing at the exchange.

'Your sister's welcome. You both come to my house,' the girl suggested.

'How'd you know she's my sister?' Reed asked in quick surprise.

'Manner. And there is a certain, familial look.'

'Hmmm. Yeah, well, that's as maybe. But the horses ain't goin' to water and feed 'emselves, ma'am.'

'No, quite,' Miss Gilkicker said precisely, and looked at Mina. 'Well, when you've finished. My house is at the end of town . . . the other end, that is. It's the one with a garden out front.'

Mina smiled indulgently, took Reed's reins as he stepped down. For a moment, she watched her brother as he set off down the sidewalk, street-side to the girl.

Reed held a puzzled silence, which neither he nor Catherine Gilkicker decided to break. The house was adobe, standing alone in an island of primroses and bluebonnet lupins. Reed hadn't seen such growing colour since leaving Lawrence eight years previously.

The girl unlocked the door. She stepped inside and held the door for Reed who pulled off his hat and ducked his head. She indicated an overstuffed chair and Reed sat with his arms and legs drawn close.

'I could make some tea, if you want. I know *I'd* like a cup,' she said.

'Yes, ma'am. Tea would be real nice. Thank you.'

The girl made a little noise of approval, said she'd only be a moment and disappeared through a door to the back of the house. Reed gave the room the benefit of his unaccustomed eye, didn't learn much in the few minutes the girl was gone.

Catherine Gilkicker returned holding a wooden tray. There was a teapot, two cups in saucers and a small bowl. 'No cream, but there's sugar, Mr. . . ?'

'I'm Reed Sawyer, ma'am. I hardly know what cream is, but I'll take the sugar. Then I wish you'd get to the business o' me bein' here. I'm feelin' real uncomfortable, an' it ain't the chair.'

'Right. Well, it's obvious I need help. Someone to help me . . . a man of fortitude. From what I've just witnessed, I think maybe it's you . . . could be you.' The girl drew up a twin chair, sat to face Reed. 'That's essentially the business of you being here, Mr Sawyer. Shall I continue?'

Reed nodded, took another sip of his tea.

'Up until yesterday I had custody of a land deed. Today I don't. I want you to get it back,' she said.

'Why does that require a man o' – what was it? – fortitude?'

'It's a long story, Mr Sawyer, so I'll go with the bones of it. For two years, I have been the owner of land that's been in the Castanar-Gilkicker family since 1850.'

Reed raised a quizzical eyebrow. 'Interestin'. Go on.'

'The United States didn't get the whole of New Mexico for nothing. My grandfather was given his land as a reward for staying peaceful. A kickback for rolling over, my pa said. It's all very complicated, Mr Sawyer, and no one really understood the ramifications. However, by the time that generation had passed on, there was nothing left, other than the estate. My mother had no money, nor did my father, although he was the legal inheritor. To claim the family right would have meant a protracted legal battle that they couldn't afford.'

'Yeah, you're right, it does sound complicated. How do *you* figure?'

'My parents died of diphtheria. They weren't old. A year on, and I'd sold all that was mine . . . everything that was left me. I travelled up from Littlefield, Texas, to see if there was a way I could re-establish the inherited land rights.'

'You *had* the documents, what happened to them?'

'Stolen from here, here in the house. I was out marketing.'

'Who was it knew you had this document?'

'There was only one person.'

'Well, in that case it was them that did the stealin'. Who was it?'

'Vernon Claye,' she said, without hesitation.

Reed leaned over to put his cup and saucer on the floor beside him. 'I see. Him of street-fightin' fame,' he suggested. '*That's* why I'm sittin' here.'

'Of course. Those two things aren't exactly unconnected. Big Greasewood is Castanar-Gilkicker land. I told him that, when I first arrived in Las Vegas. He was curious of course, even courteous. Not quite so, when he saw the deed.'

'Yeah, I noticed he weren't long on civility.'

'He sneered, said it lacked provenance. He said

I was a fraudster.'

'He said *you* were a fraudster. What was he doing with his feet under the table, then?'

'My father said that rich New Englanders were the first carpet-baggers. The land wasn't being worked, so they just moved in . . . took more land than they'd ever dreamed of.'

'Well, you got to admit, it's a story alright,' Reed said.

'It's a story that's taken a long time to unfold, Mr Sawyer. But that doesn't lessen the truth of it. It's just that I can't deal with the power of Vernon Claye. I need help, and I'm *not* going to walk away.'

Reed frowned, wanted to believe the story had a ring of truth to it. He shuffled his feet around a bit. 'Perhaps you might have to, ma'am.'

'No. I'm prepared to pay for help, Mr Sawyer. I'm offering you first refusal.'

Reed smiled. 'Thank you, ma'am. So you want me to rectify my earlier mistake. You want me to go an' shoot Claye, is that it?' he asked, immediately regretting the derision.

The girl sensed it. 'No, I do not. I want you to find the deed and return it to me,' she said, smartly.

'What is the value of the deed, ma'am? I mean, its *real* value.'

'Its real value lies in its existence. More so, to anyone with an opposing claim.'

'What? There's another claim to the land, besides yours?'

'Yes. It's held by Shelby Hite.'

'Hite?' Reed repeated the name of the saloon owner with incredulity.

'Yes. That saloon's not the only thing with a false front. Hite's real purpose in being here, is to force in a claim of his own.'

'Why? How would he have a claim?'

'Pa said that vast tracts of land were given away as rewards, benefactions by the Americans *and* Mexicans. He said it was a real muddle of paper and parchment. There could be more, for all I know. I do know Shelby Hite confronted Claye about it. I'm told voices were raised.'

Reed pushed himself back in the chair, went for a little more comfort. 'I can well imagine. So, Hite has some sort of a claim to the land, does he?'

'Not if it belongs to someone else. And it does. He's hardly got stuff to go through the courts with, but he intends to force Claye out . . . one way or another.'

'Yes, ma'am. If that's the way it is, that's the way it's lookin',' Reed agreed. 'Hite was behind that gunfight today.'

'I sort of guessed that. It *would* make sense, or rather *no* sense.'

'Claye's got other family, has he, besides his daughter?'

The girl nodded. 'Yes, he's got a nephew, but *his* money's in timber. He's get a lumber camp somewhere north of Fort Union.'

Reed considered for a moment. 'Givin' it some thought, ma'am, don't you think that Hite's the one most likely to steal your claim? I mean, he wouldn't want no competitors, would he?'

'Only Vernon Claye knew about the claim. I told you, there's no one else,' the girl reminded him.

This time Reed wasn't so sure of that fact. 'If, as you say, the document's legal ... of real worth, he'd destroy it, surely?' he proffered.

'I thought of that. But first off, he'd want to know if it was genuine. He would have been a tad worried. The land was originally Spanish gifted, so an American court might decide it's to be given back. There is a precedent for that.'

Reed shifted his gaze to the window. He wondered why Mina hadn't arrived, wondered if she was listening the other side of the front door. 'Er, just one thing, ma'am: you said your father was the inheritor, before you. Well, he wasn't related to the Emperor Maximilian, was he?' The question was the other thing Reed had on his mind.

'No, Mr Sawyer. But my mother was the daughter of Bellini Castanar, one of Maximilian's *corte*.'

Reed whistled through his teeth. 'I was thinkin' those looks o' yours weren't the preserve o' New England breedin', ma'am. An' I put that kindly ... *real* kindly.'

The girl coloured a little, but she leaned forward in a definite manner. 'Thank you, I'll take it kindly,' she said. 'Now, let's cut a deal: if you will look into the theft of my deed, I'll pay you, and well.'

'Well, it's still mighty confusin', ma'am. But tell me about this deed,' he said, thoughtfully. 'What do you hope to do with it? Just supposin' I do get it back?'

'How much do you want? I'll put it in writing,' she answered, ignoring the question.

'No need for that. I'll want fifty dollars,' he said, almost offhandedly.

'I was making you a serious offer, Mr Sawyer. How much do you want?' she repeated, with a little heat.

'No offence, ma'am, but it's an awful lot if you ain't got it. An' you already said as much.'

The girl's colour deepened, and she made a sniffy cough. 'I'm sorry. I didn't expect—'

'That's all right,' Reed cut in. 'I'm already aimin' to make one hell of a lot more than your fifty dollars.'

The girl's brow crinkled. 'I don't understand,' she said.

'I'll sell it back to him.'

'You wouldn't,' she started.

'No, I wouldn't, ma'am,' Reed smiled at his tease. 'Do you know how many men Claye's got out there?'

'At Big Greasewood? Fifteen, twenty, maybe. There's some that live out at Segundo Flat.'

Having made up his mind, Reed started to get to his feet. He saw a shadow move across the window; for a second, he thought it could be Mina.

'At least gettin' in there shouldn't prove too difficult,' he said. 'The Clayes are indebted . . . said so in public.'

The girl followed him to the door. 'Could you

call me Cass? Ma'am sounds so . . . so uncommitted.'

'Yeah, I know. Same goes for me. Try Reed.'

The two were taking in their new relationship, when someone rapped briskly at the door.

That'll be Mina, Reed thought. Come to break up the party.

'I know who that is,' Cassie said, with a pinch of smile. 'Only a sister would realize such discretion.'

But it wasn't Reed's sister.

'Oh, it's you, Benton,' Cassie said, on opening the door.

The man smiled casually, took a step back when he saw Reed. 'You've got company, Cassie. I can come back,' he said.

'No, it's all right, Benton. This is Reed Sawyer,' Cassie explained. 'Reed, this is Benton Mole, Las Vegas's attorney.'

Mole held out a firm hand. He was of Reed's age, but he had fair hair and wore a dark suit. His blue eyes and open face were valuable assets for a lawyer, was Reed's immediate estimation.

'You're a stranger to these parts,' Mole said, in a quizzical but pleasant way. And he didn't appear thrown at encountering Reed in Catherine Gilkicker's parlour.

'That's right, an' I was leavin'.' Reed fixed his hat. 'Good day, ma'am . . . Lawyer Mole,' he said.

'Good day, Mr Sawyer,' Cassie, replied, 'and thank you.'

Was Benton Mole the one she'd spoken to? Reed wondered, as he eyed the flowers. Despite her protest, there was no doubting she'd told somebody about the deed. It was something to bear in mind.

Into the street, he saw Mina coming from a general provisions store. She was holding on to a carry sack, and he hurried to meet her.

'Allow me, ma'am. I'm hit by the gallant streak,' he said with a smile, and handed her a long stem of blue lupin.

On the way to the hotel, by way of the livery, Reed told of the bargain he'd struck with Catherine Gilkicker.

'I think she's straight goods, Min. I can get what *she* wants and maybe what *we* want to know, at the same time.'

'You won't get to lose sight, will you, Reed?' Mina asked.

'No, Mina. She's cut too high off the hog for me. I had tea out of a cup.'

Mina's face softened with an approving smile. 'Chalk and cheese, right enough. But there *was* something about her I liked,' she said.

5

BIG GREASEWOOD

It was late afternoon when Reed and Mina topped a rise ten miles east of Las Vegas, caught their first sight of what was now known as Big Greasewood.

'That's no greasy sack outfit,' Mina observed.

Reed nodded absently as he gigged his roan forward.

Vernon Claye had made the original Castanar house his home. There were additional south and north wings, but the main adobe building stood squat on its base of fieldstone.

There were signs of decay; horse-nettle-filled crevices, and a wasp nest clung to an overhanging edge of the roof. To one side of the front entrance, beneath a rope swing that looped down from an old cottonwood, the ground was chalky white and dust-blown hard. Just outside of the yard, a watchful coonhound opened a lazy eye, was resting up in a chair that was collapsed in straw grass and weeds.

At their approach, three people on the wide veranda broke from their conversation. Reed reined in by the steps, and touched his hat to Mercy Claye. She smiled warm recognition, respectfully waited for her father to speak.

Vernon Claye, a distinguished-looking figure in his white suit, sat in a rocking chair with a tall glass in his hand. A man stood beside him, a working man in worn clothes who'd set a watchful gaze on Reed and Mina.

The old man limped slowly to the veranda edge, and nodded stiffly.

'Good afternoon, Mr Sawyer. And you, young lady,' he added, looking at Mina. 'Please, get down.'

'Thank you,' Mina said for them both.

'I hope you will excuse my lack of gratitude this morning,' Claye asked of Reed. 'This is a different land to the one I've known. For a moment I forgot, and for that I'm sorry.'

Reed felt an immediate twinge of embarrassment at the real purpose of his visit. 'I'm sorry too, sir,' he said. 'I gave you the impression I wouldn't be holdin' you to a debt. Well, I am, sort of. I'm here to ask for a job. Me an' my sister Mina.'

Claye nodded and smiled at Mina. 'Do you or your sister know anything of bookkeeping, Mr Sawyer? The reason I ask, is that nobody here seems to have the mastery, or indeed the inclination. My papers are in a very bad state, you see.'

Reed shook his head slowly. 'Well, it ain't exactly *my* strong suit, sir. I've done little else other than work the land. I did some soldiering of course, a few years back. But I guess there ain't much call for that out here,' he added, unnecessarily. 'But Mina can sure run a pen down numbers, if that's what you want.'

'Yes, well perhaps my foreman can sort out some appropriate work for you. The ranch is surely big enough to accommodate that,' Claye said, looking at the man who stood beside him. 'This is Gilpin Boyle, Mr Sawyer. He'll show you to the bunkhouse,' he explained. Then to Mercy, 'Please show Miss Sawyer the house when she's ready.' He turned back to Reed. 'We'll eat at six, Mr Sawyer. We'll be expecting you and your sister.'

Mercy got quickly to her feet and came down the steps. She smiled openly at Mina, then looked to Reed. 'I'd like to thank you again, Mr Sawyer. I can't believe what happened, really did.'

'That sometimes happens afterwards, Mercy. An' twice thanks, is plenty.' Reed realized the girl was in awe of the gunfight, probably of him as well. He removed his hat courteously. 'Just glad to be there,' he said gently, happy with her touch of fluster.

Leading their horses, Mina and Reed followed Gilpin Boyle to the corral. Reed was aware of the foreman's sideways glance. They'll come now, the questions, he guessed.

'So you're the feller saved the boss's life,' he declared.

Reed nodded. 'Yep, that's me,' he said, and that was all.

They turned their horses into the corral and carried their saddles to the harness shed. As Reed went inside, he leaned in close to Mina. 'If you see or hear anythin', don't look like you know it,' he said quietly.

'Not like *you* would,' she retorted with the briefest smile.

Reed's conscience was already prickly with deception, and he didn't intend to bring violence to the Claye home. Anyway, Reed doubted that either of the men they sought would recognize Mina. He'd never got a good look at them himself, could only recollect a red-cockaded hat.

Along the side of the shed, some of the crew were using the wash bench. They appeared a little bashful, took uneasy glances at Mina.

'Go on over to the house, Min. Young Mercy's there. She'll tell you what's what. Unless you want to get cleaned up here.'

Inside the bunkhouse, several men were resting, stretched out on their bunks. Reed met the hostile stare of a man who was rolling up a pair of skin leggings. The man was big and meaty, and he snorted belligerently as he got to his feet.

'You thinkin' somethin' I ain't goin' to like, bucko?' he challenged.

'Well, you ain't ever likely to find out,' Reed said, with an inoffensive smile, and shifted his glance around the room.

This time the man's voice was plain goading. 'I seen you bring your own comforter. Hope you're goin' to share an' share alike, eh bucko?'

'They didn't forget size, when they handed out your dirty mouth, *bucko*,' Reed snapped back at him, the smile gone.

'Heh, get off the stew, Rib,' Boyle called, from his corner-room cot. 'The girl's his sister, an' they're friends o' Mr Claye. Rib's always this way with strangers. You shouldn't mind him, any,' he added for Reed.

But the man called Rib took no notice of his foreman. He sucked air through his quid-stained teeth. 'You sure you ain't heifer-branded, bucko?' he continued.

Reed closed his eyes for a moment, shook his head slowly. 'Look, you were told to can it,' he warned Rib. 'Now, I suggest you take a comforter, go find a real dark place to hide.'

But Reed's reaction was what Rib needed, what he'd been pushing for. He cursed as he lurched forward, winding up his right arm, balling his fist.

Better give him what he wants. It's a shame Mina ain't here. She'd stop it, Reed thought as he stepped forward to take his punishment. Gilpin Boyle looked up in weary resignation.

Rib dropped his right shoulder and lashed out. His fist struck home savagely and Reed's head recoiled. The force of the blow was pulverizing and brought instant darkness. The sickness gripped him, but he shook it off, met Rib with a short, solid hook.

The effect wasn't as Reed had hoped, and Rib piled on into him. He was forced back, taking some of the blows on his forearms. Reed lost his footing, went down on one knee. Rib backed off, let drive with a booted foot. The blow was intended to crack Reed's chest, would have, if it had landed. Reed rolled down and caught Rib's heel. He surged back, wrenched Rib to the floor.

The men kicked themselves apart, got back to their feet. Reed was gasping, sucking in great glugs of air. He withstood Rib's charge, threw his fists in short hacking blows. Rib's head shuddered but his legs held out, drove him on. He landed a heavy right, then a sharp left that dropped Reed to the floor again.

As Rib clomped in, Reed saw the gleeful grin. He turned quickly, fell against a gate-legged table. He grabbed it, swung it out in front of him as Rib pitched forward.

There was a dull thud, and an immediate spurt of blood from the side of Rib's head. The man groaned and reeled dizzily, gave Reed time to gain his feet. Reed ducked and dived, awaited Rib's charge. It came suddenly, but Reed had measured his swing, drove in fast and hard with his right hand. The blow sent a shock wave into his chest, but together with Rib's forward rush it was the final punch.

Rib's eyes glazed and his legs wobbled. He fell heavily to the ground and lay there face down, his big body trembling, trying to get itself up.

Reed stepped away and licked his lips, wiped a trace of blood across his face with the back of his hand. 'Thought you couldn't get blood from turnips,' he snuffled.

Outside, he poured some water over his head at the wash bench, pulled away spluttering and blinking. 'That goddamn sister o' mine ain't ever around when I need her,' he said to Gilpin Boyle.

'Seems to me, you don't exactly *need* anyone,' the Big Greasewood foreman said, but not unkindly. 'I can't say how Rib is goin' to take this. It ain't happened before.'

From the dining-table, Reed smiled superficially. Knowing there was something that had to be said, his gaze flitted indifferently to the trimmings of the room. Through the arms of a wrought table candelabra he caught a sneaked wink and a nod from his sister, realized that Vernon Claye was talking to him.

'Where's home to you and Mina, Reed? Your parents' home,' the old man asked, as he refilled Reed's glass.

'Lawrence, Kansas. Ma an' Pa are both dead. Rebel guerrillas killed 'em for fifty cents an' a bag o' corn,' he added, with a dash of bile.

'Perhaps we should talk about somethin' else,' Claye's nephew suggested.

Reed's first thought on meeting Elias Claye was that the Claye strain had been undermined. Elias was on a visit to organize the ranch's turnover, bear out the paperwork. But it didn't hold his interest, and he obviously hadn't been of much help to his uncle.

Reed toyed with his wineglass, again doubted the chance of Athol Cade or Dawse Packman being anywhere near. And that meant it was only Cassie Gilkicker's business to be dealt with. He readied himself for what he had to say. He didn't think stealing deeds was Elias Clay's game. In fact, he thought that he, himself, was the only cheat sitting at the table.

'Mr Claye,' he started, after a little throat clearing. 'I was talkin' to someone of your acquaintance today. Catherine Gilkicker.'

Claye lifted a napkin, dabbed it thoughtfully at his lower lip. 'Yes, I know Miss Gilkicker. What of it?'

'One of the reasons I mention it, is because she says *she's* the owner of this here land. Got a deed to prove it. She says it was land she inherited through her father, her maternal grandfather before that. A Señor Castanar.'

'That's what she told me, yes,' Claye rumbled. 'What business is that of yours, Mr Sawyer?'

'It's the *other* reason I mention it. The deed's been stolen from her, and she's hired me to find it.'

'I see. So that's what you're really doing here.'

'Yeah. It's not the work I'm seekin'.' With that admission, Reed avoided his sister's look.

The old man go to his feet, turned an icy glare on Reed. 'I'll fall short of thanking you for your candour, Mr Sawyer,' he said. 'Now, I'd like you both to leave my ranch.'

Reed let out a breath of resignation, because it was what he'd expected.

'Father,' was Mercy's instinctive reaction, 'if

what you think is right, you're *both* being deceived by Miss Gilkicker. Mr Sawyer's just told you the truth of it. You can't throw it back in his face,' she added severely.

'How much did she pay you, Mr Sawyer? How much to intrude upon my home?' Claye continued.

Reed wanted to tell Claye what he and Mina knew about the violation of homes, but he said, 'Fifty dollars,' quietly.

Mercy looked angrily at her father, then at Reed. He gave her a shake of the head, saw that Mina was already on her feet. He glanced at Elias Claye, wasn't mistaken at the curious, complacent smirk. It immediately puzzled him, but he forgot it as he left the parlour. He lifted his hat from the stand alongside the main door, heard Mercy come up behind him and turned to face her.

'I'm sorry,' she told him. 'I guess being old's not much of an excuse. Have you ever been eighteen, Mr Sawyer?'

Reed smiled. 'No, never,' he said, and moved out through the doorway to look for Mina.

'He'll calm down, you see. He'll remember you saved his life . . . told him the truth. Are you staying in Las Vegas?' Mercy asked, calling after him.

It was well into dark when Reed followed Mina from the house, across the Big Greasewood yard. I boxed us up good and proper there, he told himself. Then he wondered why Elias Claye was down from his lumber camp, and why the smugness.

As Mina walked towards the corral, Reed pushed up the latch to the bunkhouse door. He swung it open, blinked against the pungent atmosphere, and brightness of the lamplight. Some of the crew were sprawled in their bunks, others were mending tack or playing cards, one was reading. They all turned to look as Reed stepped into the room. Rib spat noisily into a can.

Gilpin Boyle got laboriously to his feet and stiff-legged it to the door.

'Didn't think you'd last this long,' he said with a lazy smile and held out his hand. 'Good luck. An' thanks again for what you did in town. Claye's a crusty old bird, but he's a fair employer.'

Reed listened, picked up a saddle pouch that he'd left on a chair by the hay burner.

'Shame your sister can't get to look at the books, though,' Boyle continued. 'I reckon that. . .' But the man shrugged his shoulders without finishing. 'See you around,' he said finally.

'Yeah, maybe.'

In the harness shed, Mina waited for Reed to fasten his saddle.

'What did they say?' she asked.

'Nothin'. But I'm sure Boyle was goin' to say somethin' about Claye's nephew.'

'What do we do now?'

'Go back to town,' Reed said grimly. 'Tell Cassie what I learned. Then we go after Cade an' Packman.'

'You'll have to tell *Cassie* what you *reckon*. In case you forgot, Reed, you never learned a thing. And talking of faces, what you been doing to yours?'

'It was men's stuff. Someone else thought they were the big *tamale*,' Reed laughed, threw in a painful-looking grin.

6

DEEP TROUBLE

Catherine Gilkicker sat in one of her overstuffed chairs beside an oil lamp, working on a small, colourful tapestry. Close by, Benton Mole shifted his weight restlessly on the matching chair.

' "Much talk, little thought", my schoolteacher used to say. So you sure must have a lot on your mind, Cassie,' he said.

Cassie looked up with a drifting smile. 'Oh, everything and nothing, you know. I'm sorry, Benton.'

'Something to do with Reed Sawyer, I'll wager.'

Cassie stopped her work. 'As a matter of fact, it is,' she said. 'I was wondering what I could be responsible for.'

Mole smiled. 'We just about got to say hello. But I'd say he's a man who can take care of himself.

He'll find your title deed too, if Claye has it.'

'Don't you think he has it, Benton? I mean, who else could it possibly be?'

'That's conjecture, Cassie, you know that,' Mole said; then, after a moment of thought, 'You wouldn't be thinking . . . would you?'

'I *said* what I was thinking, Benton. Who else could it be?'

Mole flinched at Cassie's directness. 'Yes. Yes of course,' he said uncomfortably. 'It's just that *I'm* the only one who knew where you actually kept it. So, naturally, if you've got any doubts or suspicions. . . .'

Cassie smiled slowly, continued her needlework. 'I told *you*, because I trusted you. If I can't do that of an attorney, then I *am* in deep trouble. You're also my only friend here. The person who stole the deed, came searching for it. They'd have found it easy enough. It was in the cookie jar, for goodness sake.'

Mole nodded compliantly. Shortly after Catherine Gilkicker had arrived in Las Vegas, they'd met professionally. But they were young people of similar interests, and had gravitated together socially.

Mole pushed himself up from his chair. He circled behind Cassie and stood looking down at her for a moment. He set the tips of his fingers lightly on her shoulders. 'Cassie,' he started to say.

She gave the slightest of twitches, and immediately he took his hands away.

'It's getting late,' she said, tugging a thread.

Her response hurt Mole's self-esteem. 'Cassie, this really ain't fair,' he complained. 'You know I want more than just talk. I was hoping you felt the same.'

Cassie said nothing, and the inference was clear.

'Ah, never mind, you're on the shortfall,' he said, turning away.

'Goodnight, Benton,' was Cassie's singular, cool response.

Away from the house, Mole stopped to light himself a small cigar. In restive mood, he sucked and puffed for a full minute.

'John Brown's body's got more heat than that goddamn maiden,' he said, none too quietly. Still, now was as good a time as any to break off the relationship, he eventually decided. It was also as good a time as any to check on that deed.

Downstreet, he went to the darkened building at the rear of the hardware store where he had his office. In Las Vegas, low premiums were placed on an attorney's services. It was of a time, and a land, where law was generally .44 calibre. To one side of the low step, a dead beat old dog lay. It was partial to not liking Mole and snarled its displeasure. Then it sloped away to avoid the lawyer's boot.

In weak, yellow lamplight, Mole unlocked a desk drawer and pulled out a manila-wrapped packet. His blue eyes rolled, as he carefully spread out the aged document on his desk. The wording of the deed had been delicately penned, now mostly faded to near illegibility. At the bottom was a row of attached seals, one of them bearing the seal of Maximilian, another of the family Castanar. It was of an impeccable source, and by its holding, Mole was headed for the state bench. He'd have to play his hand right though, seek to coerce *and* be lucky.

A while ago, he'd decided that Shelby Hite was the man to watch over the land claims. Hite was a shrewd and unscrupulous operator, knew that Vernon Claye wouldn't be holding on to Big Greasewood. Hite would eventually move in, and that would be the time to present him with the original bona fides. Mole had the sure way to make Hite pay heavily for the document. After all, the Gilkicker claim was just. The bearer posed the threat to Hite, be it Benton Mole or Catherine Gilkicker.

Mole carefully refolded the deed and slipped it into his coat pocket. As an afterthought, he lifted a .32 pistol from the drawer and placed that too in his pocket.

At the livery, he waited while Levy, the hostler, saddled up his sure-foot mare. Then, in anticipation, he took the dirt road from town.

It was nearly two hours later, from the workers' township of Segundo Flat, that Mole left the girl with a dry tear.

'Bet you got more time for that lush-assed woman, eh Ben?' she said. 'Well, I jus' decided I ain't got room for your cheese bean no longer. There's other men in Vegas that'll . . .' But the girl had no need to finish her threat, because Mole had turned his back, was already walking away.

'*Adios, amigo,*' she whispered, bitterly.

Mole felt a twinge of guilt, wanted to tell her how wrong she was. But the feeling went, and he mounted up, trotted his horse back towards town. God damn all them women, he thought. With the recent turn of events, he was excited by other stuff, his head now filling with eager speculation.

As he neared the north fork junction of the town road, the sound of two horses approaching from the south made him pull off into a dry, brush-filled seep. He peered into the darkness, thought the big one riding a roan was Reed Sawyer.

Mole waited for several minutes before following on. The night wasn't that cold, but he shivered uncontrollably. What had brought Sawyer back to town, at this time of night? Could he have learned something from Vernon Claye? Something that pointed the fearful finger at him?

Later, as he rode down the deserted main street, Mole saw Reed again. He'd passed up the hotel, on his way from the livery barn. He'll be goin' to see Catherine Gilkicker, he thought. This late visit must mean he'd found something. The attorney turned into the side shadows off the street, seriously bothered, rode through back alleys to the livery.

Reed was heading for Catherine Gilkicker's house. He saw the light from a front window, was suddenly undecided because of the lateness. 'He who hesitates...' he mumbled to himself, brushing a hand at the lupins. He tapped at the door, decisive, but not loud. Cassie answered at once. She was alert, dressed as someone who'd been sitting up, waiting for something to happen.

'Reed,' she said, stepping back and aside. 'Come in, there's coffee left.'

'No thanks, ma'am ... Cass,' he said, taking off his hat. 'Me an' Mina, we've been out to Big Greasewood.'

'And?' Cassie asked eagerly. 'What did you find out?'

'Well, it weren't so much findin' out; it was more like weighin' up whether Vernon Claye's a thief or not.'

Cassie nodded perceptively. 'And you think *not*, eh Reed?'

'I didn't think you'd understand, Cass, an' I can't take your dollars.'

'I think you went to reinforce *your* doubts ... not *mine*,' she cut in, clearly annoyed. 'But if your mind's made up – and I'll wager you're not a man to change it – I'll bid you a very early good morning.'

Reed admired the resolute set of Cassie's mind, her stubbornness. 'Look,' he said intently, 'give this a sideways look. How well do you know Lawyer Mole?'

'That's none of your business ... the *other* business.'

'No, ma'am. But please think on it.' Reed put

his hat back on, tugged the brim down hard. 'An' if you change your mind, me an' Mina's takin' rooms at the hotel,' he said, as he walked from the room.

7

THE TALISMAN

Benton Mole rode through the wide, pulled-back doors of the livery, was into the barn before he stepped down from the saddle. To one side of the stalls, pulling at the straps of a saddle pouch, stood the person who'd ridden in with Reed Sawyer.

Aware of Mole's arrival, Mina turned slowly. In the lamplight she looked into the man's face, stared for a long moment unable to move, held by the blue eyes.

'Where's Levy? Who are you?' Mole asked, sensing the fearful finger.

'My name's Mina Sawyer,' Mina said, her heart thumping. 'The last time you an' me met I was a kid on a farm. It was just outside of Lawrence, Kansas, an' you tried to stick a sabre through me. My ma and pa were already dead, my sister died later. They were all of me an' Reed's family.'

Shock clawed its way up Mole's throat. No, not

after all this time, he thought, as the flush of those gory years suddenly engulfed him. 'Reed? Reed Sawyer?' he uttered disbelievingly. 'But he's the one working for Miss Gilkicker. I met him.'

Mina almost spat her words. 'He got sidetracked. It's you we came for.' She reached out her hand and eased it through the flap of the saddle pouch, felt the old, deep ache in her side as her fingers closed around the grip of her Navy Colt. 'You don't look quite the same without that tangle o' facial hair. But you're one of 'em all right. You'll be Cade, or is it Packman?'

From experience, Mole had recognized the anger, the look of reprisal, and he'd sprung forward. His hands closed around Mina's arm and he wrenched it from the saddle pouch. Mina was clutching the gun, and Mole's eyes smouldered with an almost forgotten blood lust.

'Out here, you only get one chance, little lady, an' you just passed up on it,' he scethed. 'After all these years, you shoulda shot me straight off. Shoulda shot Lieutenant Dawse Packman.'

Mina gasped with alarm, twisted the barrel of the gun around till it pointed at Mole's throat. She jerked at the trigger, cried out with frustration as Mole's hand overpowered her grip. Their bodies were buffeted, blasted from their closeness by the explosion. For the shortest moment neither of them was aware who'd taken the bullet. Then Mina shuddered, and her Colt dropped to the hard-packed floor. She went down as if in slow motion, her eyes nailing hatred into the soul of the man known as Benton Mole.

'Sweet Jeeesus.' Levy was standing in the entrance of his livery, shocked motionless by what he saw.

Mole backed off. 'The killin's weren't *all* down to me, you little spitfire,' he gabled, then turned, stumbling towards his horse. The mare was stamping its forelegs, but Mole got a toe in the stirrup. He shouted and kicked the animal into a run, was on the street before he sat the saddle.

Reed Sawyer was turning into the street from Catherine Gilkicker's when he heard the gunshot. He saw a rider swerve out from the livery, kicking at a big horse, urging it from town at on all-out gallop.

Dread gripped at Reed's vitals and he started to run. Pain was tearing at his chest as he arrived breathless at the doors of the livery.

The hostler was bending over a sprawled form, and Reed ran straight on through. He shoved Levy aside. 'Mina,' he called desperately.

'The girl's hurt real bad, mister,' the hostler whispered. 'I was back gettin' some coffee ... heard the shot ... saw *him*.'

Reed grabbed the man by his neck collar and twisted it savagely. '*Him*? Who the hell was *him*? Tell me.'

'I can't, you're chokin' me ... I ...'

Reed loosened his grip and the hostler rubbed his throat. 'It was the lawyer ... Mole,' he rasped. 'He shot her real close ... ran when he saw me.'

Reed dropped to his knees beside Mina and turned her gently towards him. His hand was warm and tacky from the blood, but there was little of it. Then he felt the lump to one side of her stomach. It was the Apache love doll, mashed up by the bullet, but its charm had worked.

'She's alive, goddamnit. She's only still livin'. Go get a doctor,' he yelled at Levy. 'Find a gun o' some sort. Use it, if he needs persuadin'.'

Reed's attention was brought round to the approach of Shelby Hite and a few men who were gathering behind him. Hite frowned, twisted the end of his long, wispy beard.

'You know who did this?' he asked with seeming concern.

'It was Benton Mole,' Reed rasped. 'An' if I thought the warnin' you gave me had led to this, I'd kill you where you stand.'

Hite backed away from Reed's unstable anger. 'The lawyer?' he said. 'And you think *I'd* be involved in a killin' like this?'

'From what I already seen o' you, yeah, I think that's possible. Now get out o' my way. I ain't waitin' for any sawbones.'

Reed carefully gathered Mina in his arms, didn't look at Hite or the others as they cleared his way. He turned along the sidewalk, but halted after a few steps. What now? What next? he thought emptily.

Then suddenly Catherine Gilkicker was alongside him, the whites of her eyes bright in the moonglow.

'I'm so sorry, Reed,' she said softly. 'Take her to my house. The doctor will come there. Please.'

After a few minutes' walk he went into the house and into the bedroom, laid Mina's unconscious body on Cassie's bed. He stood there a long time, until his mind started to serve him again and he realized that Cassie was talking to him.

'If, for one moment, I thought that what I asked of you, had *anything*—'

'I don't know what you're about to come up with, but it was Benton Mole who shot Mina, an' I don't believe we're talkin' chance here.' As Cassie's jaw dropped, Reed continued. 'Can you make sure she gets what's needed, take care o' her? First thing she'll try an' do, when she comes round, is come after me. An' I ain't forgot your trouble, Cassie. It's just that I got a priority ... always did have. I'll be gone for a while.'

As Cassie stood in shocked silence, Reed walked past her to the door. He nodded his thanks as he went out, and didn't look back.

'Why? Can you tell me why?' Cassie called after him.

Reed resaddled his roan at the livery, was cantering along the south road before his confused mind caught up with Cassie's question. It was a good one. Why should a young lawyer ruin all his new found opportunities by committing murder? Well, Reed reckoned he had the answer. Las Vegas's attorney wasn't all he seemed. He wouldn't have brought about the shooting, and there was only one reason for Mina to. She'd recognized him.

She'd seen him as the person she remembered, and that wouldn't have been Benton Mole.

Reed considered Athol Cade, then ruled him out, shifted the description they had of Dawse Packman on to the face of Mole. Without the wisps of yellow beard, he reckoned he'd caught up with the one-time Kansas Bushwhacker. It was a remarkable coming together of the ways, an evil serendipity, that Benton Mole should be the guerrilla thief and murderer who had ridden on to the Sawyer farm, five long years ago.

8

REUNION

Benton Mole reached the Big Greasewood ranch house an hour after midnight. For fear of being seen, or sniffed out by an untamed pack of dogs, he'd pulled off the road well short of Segundo Flat. He swung wide on the moonlit grassland, rode in from the west side to a dense, cottonwood brake. He'd almost killed his mount in his haste to get there, and he ran a hand over its glistening flank, listened to its broken, laboured breathing.

Mole doubted Las Vegas would find anyone to hunt him, or even get out a dodger, but it was of little consolation. He knew Reed Sawyer would likely follow him to hell and forever. All he had was the clothes he was wearing, his pocket pistol and a stove-up horse. He had no food and needed help, fast.

He left the cottonwoods and gave the corrals, outsheds and bunkhouse a wide berth. At the main house, all windows were dark, except for a solitary light burning in a ground-floor window of the south wing. The man never did sleep. That'll be his room, he thought confidently, and made his way around the perimeter of the yard.

Carefully, Mole edged up to the side of the lighted window, looked in to see Elias Claye sitting alone in an high-backed leather chair. Mole tapped his fingers against the glass, and Claye turned, pulled off his reading glasses. He came to the window, his mouth working at silent oaths and epithets as he recognized the lawyer.

Mole signalled for him to open the window, and Claye eased up the sash.

'Move out the way,' Mole said, hanging a leg over the sill. He stepped into the room and closed the window, turned to appreciate the polished oak and rich furnishings.

'What it is to have family, eh, Captain?' he said.

'Keep your mouth down, and don't call me that,' Claye hissed. 'I told you never to come here. What do you want?'

'This Sawyer don't know me from spit,' Claye said, when Mole was finished with telling him.

Mole shook his head doubtfully. 'Well, I just got through shootin' his sister. I didn't fully mean to, but I did. I reckon they both got our likenesses . . . carry 'em in their heads. Right now, you're no more safe than I am. You got to get me some clothes an' a fresh horse. An' I need money.'

'Why should that concern me?'

Mole regarded Claye with concern. 'Listen,

Mister Captain, whatever you want to call yourself. Sure it's been five years, an' we both grown some. But those Sawyers didn't get here by chance. There was three of us left. So what if they caught up with Neavis Tripp?'

'How would Tripp know where to find us?' Claye demanded.

Mole laughed scornfully. 'He always knew where we were. It wouldn't ever have been in his interest to say anythin', an' he never did. Unless, of course, Sawyer did find him. Then he'd have talked.'

'But it was only the girl could identify us. And if she's dead. . . ?' Clay put forward.

Mole's face muscles tightened with impatience. 'I can see how you never made general,' he rasped angrily. 'The hostler saw me shoot her. So Sawyer – who's her brother remember – is goin' to be breathin' down my neck any moment. You're only safe until he gets here. Then he's goin' to be breathin' down *your* neck. Now, I reckon *that's* a fur-trimmed, Jim Dandy reason for you getting' me that stuff.'

Claye turned on Mole, as the years of freedom and haven suddenly started to burn. 'I should have shot you before we ever left Kansas.'

'Yeah, well, it's too late now, Captain. Of course, we could both sit here an' wait for Sawyer. I mean, he's bound to be in one hell of a convivial mood.'

Claye cursed him, then went to a writing desk. 'I'll give you a hundred dollars, and a note that's good for four hundred more. There's a place in the mountains about ten miles north of Fort Union.'

'Are you talkin' about your lumber camp?'

Claye nodded. 'Yeah, where I should have stayed. It'll be safe enough. The low life that work there, aren't goin' to say much; they'll even lie for you. Look for Rufus Ockley. He'll pay you, sort you out a bunk an' some food. Give him back fifty of the hundred.'

'Have you got a coat? I'll freeze up in that country.'

'I saw some blanket coats pegged out back. Take one of them.'

'I need something to eat now.'

'Eat worms for Chris'sake. You've had all you're getting from me. Now get yourself back out that window.'

'I'm going.' Mole hesitated, then drew the packeted deed from his outside jacket pocket, transferred it to an inside one.

'What's that?' Claye asked.

'Nothin'.'

'It's something I'm supposed to see, goddamnit. What is it?'

Mole gave a sly grin. 'It's the deed I borrowed from Catherine Gilkicker. It crossed my mind for a moment that you might have a use for it. It don't involve any work, so how much would it be worth, Captain?'

'It's worthless,' Claye said with a derisive snort. 'The Gilkicker woman tried to take old Vernon with it. It's worth less than shinplaster.'

'Well, that's not my opinion, so I'll just hang on to it for a bit longer. Maybe I'll return when I can use it,' Mole suggested.

Claye studied him for a chilly, silent moment. 'You be *real* careful, if an' when you do,' he threatened. 'You came here on a horse, I suppose?'

'Yeah, I left it in the cottonwoods. It's near windbroke.'

Claye nodded. 'Get back there. Get unsaddled and wait. I'll find you a fresh one from the corral.'

'Get me a good runner, Captain. Remember, neither of us wants Sawyer to catch up with me.'

9

RUNAWAY TRAIL

Reed Sawyer cursed quietly. From hunkering down, he stretched himself, shifted against the sweaty cling of his shirt. It was an hour after sunrise, and his legs ached from looking close at road trails that were still muddied from the recent big rain.

He wiped his sleeve across his face, puffed tiredly with exasperation. Reed wasn't a tracker, and in a dark, watery moonlight it had been difficult spotting Mole's fresh trail. But he'd learned the track was making straight for Big Greasewood, though. And now, early light him found well into their land.

It was clear that Mole had pushed his own mount hard, and was still many hours ahead. But Reed remounted the roan and went slowly on, leaning from his saddle to keep an eye on the road.

Coming up from the grassland ahead, a grey cow pony caused him to stop and loosen one of the two guns he now carried. A minute later, it was Mercy Claye who touched stirrups alongside.

The girl's face was colouring up, and she avoided his eyes as she removed her hat. 'I ride the early morning . . . most mornings,' she started to explain.

But Reed cut in impatiently. 'Do you know Lawyer Mole? Benton Mole?' he asked.

'Yes,' she said, turning to face him. 'By sight.'

'Have you seen him?'

'This morning? Hardly. Should I have, this early?'

'He shot Mina last night. She's barely alive, an' I'm lookin' for him.'

'The lawyer Mole shot your Mina? Why on earth? I don't understand.'

'No, you wouldn't, Mercy, an' I've no time to explain. Just believe me.'

'I'll listen,' Mercy said, without hesitation.

'Mole's tracks lead to your ranch. I've been followin' 'em most o' the night.'

She shook her head. 'No. He couldn't. I would have known.'

'Where would he go from here? Assumin' he did come by.'

'What, from here? I don't know. Segundo Flat? The lumber camp? I guess if he wanted to stay out of the way . . . yes, he'd go there. But that's Elias's. You don't think. . . ?'

Reed was staring into the distance. 'I don't know

what to think this moment, Mercy. Tell me how he'd get there, who he'd see.'

'Thanks,' he said simply, when she'd told him. He started to turn the roan's head away, but she reached out and caught his arm, her face losing some of its colour.

'I'll talk to Pa; get some help. You can't go alone, not up there.'

'That's exactly how I've got to go, Mercy.'

'Well, just be . . . just be . . .'

'Careful?' Reed offered with a smile. 'Yeah, I will.' Then he rode away, the brief tenderness already forgotten.

At first dark, Reed rode through the last of the down timber, sniffed the soft vanilla of the mighty bull pine. He saw the cluster of shacks that was the base of Elias Claye's logging camp, a quarter-mile ahead. In ten minutes, he dismounted in front of a low, clapboarded building where a burned-in sign said PONDEROSA. A cow pony was tied at the rail, but it wasn't the sure-foot mare the livery man had told him was Benton Mole's.

Reed stepped into what looked like the camp's general store, meeting place and bar. Two loggers turned from their table, gave an almost hostile stare as he came in. He ignored them, looked across at the man who pushed aside a greasy plate to make an entry in a ledger. He was big-gutted, wore dark pants and a dirty vest. His eyes stayed unreadable in a tangle of dark hair and whiskers.

'You Ockley?' Reed asked him.

'Rufus Ockley.' The man's voice was short and breathy, like one of his rip-saws.

Reed noticed he wasn't asked his own name. 'I'm lookin' to bed down for a couple o' days,' he said. 'An' the roan needs a stall.'

'If you say so. You wanna drink?'

Reed nodded, and Ockley set out a glass, pulled a bottle from under the short run of bar he was standing at. The big measure drained the bottle and Ockley used it to rap twice against the back wall, as Reed snapped a coin on to the bar top.

'There's some burgoo left; you wanna plate?' he asked Reed.

'Anythin',' Reed said, and Ockley went round him and out the door. Reed heard him walking the roan to its stabling, was glad he had nothing of value or identifiable in his saddle traps.

Twenty minutes later, Ockley returned. He pushed his hand through an open window of an annexed kitchen, drew out a plate of potatoes and deer meat, which he handed on to Reed.

It was only while he was forking down the food that Reed pondered on the dirty plate and Ockley's tap on the adjoining wall. There was someone else here he thought. Someone who'd arrived not long before. Benton Mole had certainly ridden to Big Greasewood for something. The lumber camp was owned by one of the Clayes, so if Mole was here, it made Rufus Ockley a worry; and Reed started to.

Beyond the heavily dusted windows, night had pressed down from the Cristos. Ockley had brought in some stove lengths that he used to fill the stove. He didn't say anything to Reed. It really was as though he didn't want to get involved.

As the room warmed, Reed realized it was thirty-six hours since he and Mina had broken camp with Herran Tudor and young Cawden Fisher. All that had happened since seemed unreal, a drift of nightmare scenes that told mostly of his weariness. He looked across at Ockley. No, I'm not sleepin', you lard gut, he thought. Whatever's on your mind, think again. But it was Reed's thinking that made him ask about his space for the night.

'Through the back; there's two rooms. You take the one on the right,' the man told him plainly.

Reed tossed his hat on to the dark shadow of his cot, swore as he knocked a shin getting to the window. He twisted the latch and pushed, shuddered at the inrush of chilly mountain air. He turned and stared at the room's adjoining wall, wondered if he was less than six feet from Lieutenant Dawse Packman. Then, settled in the darkness to wait, he huddled deeper into his coat, lay down on his back with a matched Navy Colt in each hand.

10

ATTORNEY'S END

The spare buildings of the Ponderosa camp were flanked by towering stands of pine. Through it ran the lumber road, and now, propped on his elbows, Reed could see it like a hoary ribbon in the moonlight.

Then he was on his feet, listening to the shallow creak and groan of a room's door hinges. 'Christ, he's leavin',' he mouthed silently. 'It's him, Packman.' Reed's nerves were taut with the need to follow; the impulse of a five-year quest.

Think, think, think. Stay here. he told himself. Remember that Ockley don't like me. He's probably outside right now, covering Packman's back. He's watchin' the window, watchin' the door, waitin' to put some bullets in me.

Reed shoved one of the Colts into his holster, the other he held out, levelled its barrel through the open window and drew back the hammer. For a long two minutes he stood motionless, steely patient until he heard the dull knock of hoofbeats.

The horse was a dark chestnut, and it broke into its run the moment it left the stable off to Reed's right. It wasn't the clear-footed mount that the lawyer had ridden from Las Vegas, but from thirty feet, Reed fired into the night. The horse shuddered, tossed its head in a wild arc, and Reed went for a second shot.

Benton Mole lost control of the panicked horse almost immediately. He dragged his feet from the stirrups and fell, went into a rolling slump. He pulled himself to his hands and knees, stubbornly shook his head. He felt for his small calibre pistol, wished for his old Sharps carbine.

Reed didn't fire again. No, not yet, he told himself. He knows where Athol Cade is. I've got to let him live for a bit.

'There's nowhere to go, Mole,' Reed yelled. 'All your runnin's done.'

The will to survive, to fight on, was still strong and Mole found his gun. He rolled into a sitting position and fired almost blind at the window. Then he was on his feet, racing for tree cover as his bullet spat into the weathered frame of Reed's window.

Reed brought his Colt to bear on Mole's legs. He shot carefully and missed, and Mole vanished into the timber. 'Real smart,' he seethed. 'Keep him guessin', let him live for a bit by lettin' him get clean away.'

With a vicious curse, Reed kicked open his room

door, went fast through the bar and store room. In the doorway, Ockley turned to challenge him, the outline of his scattergun sharp against the blue darkness. Reed didn't falter, went on to hit the big belly with his lifted knee. It was too fast for Ockley, and he went down with an agonizing wheeze. Reed stepped on the man's back and was away into the road.

But Mole was back, and Reed saw his shadow against the open door of a tool shed. He crouched, moved backwards against the logged braces of the building. There was a flash and a pulse of air as Mole's second bullet scythed past him into a sorghum barrel. Reed was up then and running fast, slanting across the road. He made the front of the shed, stood hard-pressed against the door wall. From inside, Mole shot again and Reed moved sideways, firing into the deep dark, then again, as he took a rolling dive inside.

His shoulder buffeted a rickety partition, and he went down with the splintering timbers, landed with a winded grunt. For a moment he lay still, then he rolled on to his side in the stinking crust of oil and shavings. He could see and hear very little, other than a few stars through a hole in the roof, a horse that sounded like his roan whickering at the gunfire.

Reed pushed the Colt deep into his pocket, pulled the second from his holster. He drew back the hammer and with his nervy reflex, Mole fired at the sharp metallic sound. The bullet ricocheted off the hanging blade of a rip-saw, missed Reed's face by less than a foot. There was a noise at the back of the shed and, closing his eyes, Reed took a calculated shot into the darkness ahead of him.

The noises continued and, as Reed's eyes got accustomed to the dark, he saw the crouching shape that moved itself low down into a far corner of the shed. Yeah, that's it, he's hunkerin' down, expects me to go forward to flush him out, he speculated. He'll wait until I'm up close, then fire point blank. But I been countin' an' you've used four shots, Packman. Let's see if we can make it more, he decided.

Reed took a deep breath and stepped sideways, his back framed against the open doorway. Then he moved forward tentatively and grabbed for the other Colt. He drew the hammers on both guns, threw himself behind a packing crate the moment Mole fired his fifth shot.

'I reckon that's it, Packman,' he called out anxiously. 'Five shots. You rebel cavalry always rode on a dead chamber.'

Mole's bitter yell fused with the roar of his gunshot. 'Not in an army saddle any more, Sawyer. You should—'

But Mole's words were choked off as Reed's bullet hit him in the belly. Coming up and out of the corner, Mole bent double, then stumbled forward a pace before going down.

'I've goddamn killed him,' Reed muttered. He pointed the barrel of his Colt towards the body, moved forward two, then three paces. 'Don't you die on me, Packman,' he rasped. Then he grabbed the man by his coat lapels and dragged him outside of the shed.

'You hear me, Packman? Don't you go buyin' any farm yet, you murderin' coward.'

Mole's eyes rolled and his head moved. He coughed blood, shiny black in the moonlight. 'I'm goin' 'cause you gut shot me.' His words were faltering and harsh. 'I knew you'd catch up sometime . . . just wondered where you'd been all these years.' He coughed and more blood oozed on to the dirt road. 'You wanted me alive? Well, you sure got that wrong.'

Reed knelt beside Mole. 'You'll live long enough tell me about Cade,' he said. 'Who is he? Where can I find him?'

Mole dragged up a curious, regretful smile. 'You'll never know, you son-of-a-bitch. Not now you done this.'

Reed prodded Mole's bloody wound with the tip of his Colt, watched closely as the man's face contorted in soundless agony.

'I'll keep doin' that, until you tell me,' he said brutally.

'You make sure you kill him,' Mole hissed.

'I promise,' Reed said, and smiled coercively.

'It's Elias Claye you're lookin' for.'

'Claye? *He's* Athol Cade? Vernon Claye's nephew?'

'Well, he's some sort o' shirt-tail kin. The old man never knew about his war exploits, not until it was too late. He'd been harbourin' a wanted war criminal close on a year by then. Claye gave him his own family name . . . used our booty to set him up here.' Mole made a short gulping chuckle, another rattling breath. 'It was Cade's new standin' that supported *me*. Amazin' what a suit an' half-a-dozen law books says in a town like Las Vegas.' Then his voice broke, and his eyes closed. 'Get me a drink,' he said.

'No. You're dyin', Mole, an' I want it to hurt.'

'Please.'

Reed was ready for a trick, and he turned his head to see Ockley limping towards him. The heavy man had a lantern hanging from the barrel of his scattergun.

'Go bring a bottle,' Reed told him.

Ockley nodded and shuffled away. Reed watched his back until he saw him disappear inside.

'Pity you weren't at home with the rest o' your family,' Mole croaked, his voice unexpectedly tough, and mocking. 'We coulda got us a whole nest o' Jayhawkers. Was that little spitfire really your kid sister. . . ?'

For an answer, Reed slashed Mole across the mouth with his gun barrel.

When Ockley returned, he'd left his scattergun behind, was holding a glass of whiskey instead.

Under the glow of Ockley's lantern, Reed searched Mole's pockets. He found $100 cash, a promissory note for $400 from Elias Claye, and the land deed. He examined it first, then folded it neatly and placed it deep inside his coat.

Wearily, he wondered how pleased Catherine

Gilkicker would be for its return. If he told her the whole story, she'd hardly believe it. For her own part, she wouldn't be showering him with kisses, that was a certainty.

'You want me to do anythin'?' Ockley asked, without enthusiasm.

Reed stood up and took the whiskey, poured it down on to Mole's face. 'If he's dead, bury him. If he ain't, run him feet first through the saw-mill,' he said, icily, and turned away.

11

THE NIGHT SHOOT

Early the following morning, Reed saddled his roan. Then out of curiosity he went to where Packman's chestnut mare was stalled, immediately noticed its Big Greasewood brand. Mercy Claye had told him that Packman, or Mole as she knew him, hadn't showed at the ranch. Well, that meant that Packman must have had some hush meeting with Elias Claye. And that's how he'd got the horse and the $100.

Ten minutes later, leading the chestnut mare, Reed was on the long trail back towards the Canadian River and Las Vegas. If Vernon Claye knew about his nephew's war-time identity of Athol Cade, then the horse, the money and the deed, should convince him that he was guilty of aiding and abetting not one, but two thieves and murderers.

Throughout the day, Reed rode steadily. From the timberline he skirted Fort Union, followed the contours of the land that inclined gradually for thirty miles. Eventually, deep into full dark he found himself on the immense rolling grasslands that he'd charted on his first visit out to Big Greasewood.

Two hundred yards from the main buildings of the ranch, three men were tying in their horses to a long run of snake fencing. They continued on foot, and on a word from Shelby Hite, stopped in the deep shadow of a hay barn.

Hite wiped his hand across his face, felt the nip of cold sweat between his shoulder blades. It was a few minutes off midnight, and except for a low light along the south wing of the main house, the spread lay in sleeping darkness. Hite had been through the set-up twice already, but looking at each man as though defying them to make a mistake, he went through it a final time.

'Juice, you and me, we'll handle the main house. Fijo, shore up the bunkhouse door. Use a couple of poles from the corral. Do it quick, but be quiet. Then stand back, cover the windows. There shouldn't be any trouble. If there is, they'll have to climb out, an' you'll have to shoot them. You got that?'

Fijo nodded his head once. He was of mixed blood, a Chicano whom Hite had hired to do the job. He was a quiet man, but competent, able to contain the danger of Big Greasewood's crew for an hour. Hite wasn't concerned about the citizens of Segundo Flat. Collectively, they cared little for the American landowners, wouldn't offer much in the way of loyalty or assistance unless they had to. Juice Mickens was a throwaway, a bar rat, who took Hite's orders for the price of a drink.

Fijo held the shadow darkness, as he made his way toward the corral. Mickens dutifully went along with Hite, who'd visited the ranch before. He'd come to show his old land claim to Vernon Claye. Not surprisingly, he'd been ordered off Big Greasewood land, but it had given him the chance to take note of the house and its immediate grounds.

Now, as he and Mickens skirted the north wing of the house to reach the first of the rear doors, he was hoping there'd be no hitch. If only Herran Tudor had succeeded in what he was paid to do, it would have been relatively easy to deal with Vernon Claye's daughter and his nephew. Claye was a wily old bird, and he wouldn't be suckered again, and Hite knew there'd be no chance against their wealth in any court.

Furthermore, Hite hadn't got to clear Reed Sawyer from his mind. Three nights ago in the livery, he was almost a victim of Sawyer's reprisal killing, Still, it could be worse, he thought. He could be Benton Mole, with Sawyer riding him down to the last roundup.

They'd got to the house now, and Hite indicated that Mickens put a match to the lantern he was carrying. Hite took it from him and, shielding its glow, he held it close to the door and lifted the latch. Very cautiously, he stepped through into the food store that led off the kitchen.

Taking a quick look around, Hite nodded for Mickens to follow, then he moved on. On the far side of the dining-room, the lantern flickered its light into a wide hallway with closed doors along its walls. Hite knew they were the bedrooms, and that three of them were occupied. He stood silent, considered for a moment. He guessed the girl and Elias Claye might offer token resistance, but it was Vernon Claye's wilful grit that troubled him.

Hite shuddered as a strip of light appeared from under the door nearest him. Then he heard the squeak of a floorboard. Someone was coming to the door because they'd heard something. Hite's heart thumped its beat, and he reached for the Colt he wore in a shoulder holster beneath his riding coat.

It was Vernon Claye who pulled the door wide. The old man stood there dressed in a night robe, holding out his heavy pistol. When he saw Hite, he gasped with shock, instinctively pulled the trigger against an action that he'd not set.

But Hite didn't know that. He countered by firing point blank at Claye who was standing his ground in mute astonishment. The gunshot boomed, reverberated wildly in the wood-panelled hallway. Hite swore, took a step back as Claye's frail body crumpled. The old Army Colt banged heavy as it hit the floor, and Hite was already hoping that Fijo had got the door to the bunkhouse jammed up good and tight.

The next door along the hallway was flung open

and Mercy Claye came out, clutching a long wrapper tight to her body. She saw Hite then Mickens; immediately understanding what had happened, she dropped to her knees alongside her father. Elias Claye was coming from his room at the end of the hallway and Hite took a step towards him.

Mercy sprang to her feet and, with a piercing scream, swung her father's gun at the back of Hite's head. But Mickens was quick. He punched out hard at her arm, then backhanded her across the face as she spun around. She fell soundlessly at his feet, and Hite yelled at Elias Claye.

'Make a stupid move and you'll die, mister.' As he spoke, they all heard the sound of a gunshot from somwhere across the yard. A hound started baying, and Hite was swearing again. 'Jesus, the bunkhouse,' he remembered, and looked toward Mickens who had his gun on Elias Claye. Hite chanced that Fijo had the ranch hands and the foreman's coonhound bottled up in the bunkhouse. 'Now, I want keys to these rooms,' he said, sharply.

'They'll probably be on Vernon's desk. What do you want them for?' Elias asked, fearful and drained of colour.

'Just get them,' Hite ordered.

The man shuffled across the hallway, gave his uncle's body a jumpy glance as he went into the bedroom. He opened the single drawer of a writing-table as Hite watched from the doorway.

'The keys,' Hite said. 'Nothing else.'

Claye shivered in the cold of the night and held

up the bunch of keys.

'Drag the body inside,' Hite told him. 'Get the girl back to her own room, then lock the doors . . . both doors.'

'What are you goin' to do to me?' Claye asked with genuine concern.

'Nothing. Not yet anyways. We're just goin' to talk a bit.' Hite smiled weakly, then he turned to face Fijo who'd come quietly into the house carrying a happy-jack lantern.

Fijo took in the stricken forms of Claye and Mercy. 'Did you hurt that kid?' he asked, with quiet menace.

'Don't go kicking the stall, she's not dead. Juice had to quieten her down,' Hite responded irritably, as the Chicano turned to Mickens.

'I heard shots,' Hite said. 'What happened?'

'They tried the door. One of 'em poked a gun out the window. I put a bullet up its barrel.'

Hite slowly pushed his gun back into its holster. Too late to pull back now, he thought to himself. 'You'd better get back there,' he told Fijo. 'Take Juice with you. That crew'll be busting the bunkhouse down soon.'

Fijo hesitated. 'You got things to do here in the house, eh, boss?' he insinuated.

'Yes. I'll be talking with Claye's nephew, if it's any of your business. And the girl's going to be safely locked in her room,' he added drily.

It was shortly after midnight when Reed Sawyer rode close to the dark-shadowed outbuildings of

BIG GREASEWOOD

Big Greasewood. He dismounted, talked soothings to the two horses as he hitched them in the cottonwood grove. Then he walked cautiously, took cover alongside a hay barn when he saw a light showing from the bunkhouse further on. It was late hours, even for a busy ranch, he thought, and his misgivings increased.

12

STRIKING A DEAL

Shelby Hite lit a nerve-calming cigarillo, regarded Elias Claye through the first puffs of smoke.

'I never meant to kill your uncle. I just want you to know,' he said.

'Then you shouldn'ta been here,' Claye answered back.

The two men were catercornered at the dining-room table. Claye had got himself partly dressed and, with the help of a large bourbon, he'd regained some composure.

Hite frowned. 'It's Big Greasewood I want.'

'Yeah, I already knew that. You even got yourself a paper.' Claye's tone was faintly insolent. 'You were goin' to move him an' us, all of the crew off Big Greasewood, just like that? Well, I'm guessin' you're in a tight spot, with the death of old Vernon. You'll soon be back tendin' bar in that dog hole o' yours.'

'Not yet, friend. I've still got command.'

'You ain't got a pot to piss in, *friend*. So what's it to be? Another murder, or a deal?'

Hite thought for a moment. 'And if you were me?' he asked, switching the question.

'Old Vernon was already dead, that's my story. He died o' natural causes . . . had a heart attack before you got here. At his age, it ain't stretchin' the truth too much. Nobody'll be puttin' the law on to us.'

'You're forgetting the girl.'

'I ain't forgettin',' Claye said, almost breaking into a smile. 'I've had to recast my life before this. It's just another necessity of survival.'

At Claye's cold-blooded solution, Hite wondered what Fijo's reaction would have been. Then he thought that maybe it was a ruse, that Claye was merely biding time until he could see justice meted out to his uncle's killer.

As if he understood Hite's unease, Claye fleshed-out his plan.

'When I arrived here after the war, Vernon told me his will didn't have much settin' out. He was leavin' everythin' to Mercy. Well, that weren't too much of a surprise, considerin' my war record. So, thanks to you, old Vernon's handed me the busted flush.'

'The girl's not going to deal against you: you're her kin, for God's sake,' Hite said.

'She'll do what her pa wanted her to, an' that's to keep me from owning any part o' Big Greasewood.' Claye's eyes suddenly burned with resentment. 'I'm no goddamn woodcutter, an' that goddamn will's not more'n thirty goddamn feet away from where I'm sittin'.'

Hite understood Claye's standpoint, then. 'If we held the land grant between us, we'd avoid costly legal action and there'd be no close nosing around.'

Claye chuckled. 'Yeah, that's it, feller. The precise nature o' Vernon's demise needn't go beyond this ranch. Will your men keep their mouths shut?'

'They will, if they're fed the right number of dollars. What about the Big Greasewood crew?'

'I'll pay 'em off in the mornin'. Most of 'em'll head straight for Albuquerque. There's elements o' chance, but darers go first, eh, feller?'

'First to take the pennies from dead men's eyes,' Hite said, his words full of loathing. 'I want no part of what you've got planned for the girl.'

'You won't have,' Claye told him. 'An' there's one more thing you probably don't know.'

Outside, Reed was about to move on from the hay barn, when two men suddenly appeared from around a corner of the bunkhouse ahead of him.

'Think I'll go see to the horses,' one of them said. 'It looks quiet enough here.'

'Yeah,' his partner returned. 'A kid with a corn-shooter could hold 'em in for a year.' The man had a furtive glance around him, pulled a tobacco pouch from his shirt and started to build a cigarette. Reed tried to see something of his face, but he hadn't seen much of the Big Greasewood crew and didn't know him.

'Hey, mister,' he called out softly.

'Who the hell's that? Who's there?' Fijo challenged, his hand moving towards his high-belted holster.

Reed got the hunch of something not right. 'Neighbour,' he said openly, holding up his arms. 'I know it's late, but I got urgent business with Vernon Claye.'

'You got no horse?' Fijo asked suspiciously.

'Left her out by the cottonwoods,' Reed said, which was true. 'She's a tad switchy, don't like to mix it. Can you take me to see Claye?'

'A neighbour, you say? Well, I guess that'll be all right,' Fijo said, but unconvinced, not wholly certain of his ground. He swung around as though to lead off, but Reed saw the discreet movement of his hand.

Reed drew his Colt and took a couple of long, catching-up strides. Fijo wheeled and brought up his own gun, tightened when he saw that Reed was already on him. Reed mouthed a disingenuous apology, then swung the frame of his Colt hard and fast against the side of the man's face. Fijo grunted deep, slumped forward and went down.

Reed listened for a moment, then hooked his arms under Fijo's shoulders and dragged him back to the hayshed. He let him down round the back, then returned to study the bunkhouse and the coral poles that jammed up the door. The significance was obvious, but he could only guess at why.

Keeping low, he ran diagonally across the yard to the main house. Through the rails of the veranda he noticed that only a middle room was lighted, and he went on around the north wing. He stepped lightly on to the back porch and edged along. Carefully he lifted a latch, pushed the barrel of his Colt to open the store-room door.

Inside, Elias Claye was explaining about the Gilkicker-Castanar deed, how it had got into the hands of Lieutenant Dawse Packman, aka Benton Mole.

'He even offered to sell it to me,' he told Hite.

Hite leaned across the table, dipped the wet end of his cigarillo in Claye's drink.

'How do you know it's not a fake?' he asked.

'Ha, what's a fake an' what ain't? Vernon thought it was though, so did I. No, I reckon it's about as genuine as it can be, an' that's the trouble. Its existence don't help *our* end game.'

'Only if it gets back into Catherine Gilkicker's cute little paws,' Hite said, thoughtfully. 'The courts will look more kindly on her claim. It's got Spanish provenance, an' that's a hell of a lot more original than anything in the Claye name, or anyone else's.'

'Yeah, well, we'll have to get to Packman before Reed Sawyer does,' Claye asserted, pushing away his unfinished bourbon.

The two men schemed for a while. Claye was to pay off the Big Greasewood crew and Hite said he'd take Fijo and Mickens and go after Packman.

Claye would also handle the problem of Cousin Mercy.

Both men looked up as they heard someone approaching from the kitchen. The way things stood, they assumed it would be Fijo or Juice Mickens.

13

THE RUTHLESS EDGE

Shelby Hite looked up to see the Navy Colt in Reed Sawyer's hand. His jaw dropped and the sweat immediately appeared across his temple. Reed stepped forward and relieved him of his gun. Without a word, he let the hammer down, shoved it into his belt. His turned his attention to the shocked face of Elias Claye.

'You got a short while to tell me what's goin' on here, Cade. A *very* short while,' Reed said, the menace clear in his voice.

Hite drew long and slow on his cigarillo. 'I don't know what size army you've got out there, Sawyer,' he drawled. 'But I'd put you down as someone who acts out of good sense, not recklessness.'

'I'm doin' this on disgust an' loathin', mister,'

Reed snarled. 'Now, Vernon Claye an' his daughter Mercy. Where are they?'

Hite coughed, drew an unsettled breath. 'Claye's dead. We never killed him. He had a heart seizure of some sort.'

'The girl? Where's she?'

'She's not harmed. She's in her room,' Hite answered carefully. 'I've got men with me, Sawyer,' he said. 'If there's any trouble here, they'll be over you like a blanket.'

'Yeah, right,' Reed snorted and moved his attention back to Elias Claye. Reed had learned of Claye's real identity, and he could see the fearful knowledge in the man's features. But some of the rebel bushwhacker's ruthless edge remained, and Reed could see that too, as he held the man's eyes steady.

'You caught up with Packman, then?' Claye asked of him, and stirred uneasily.

'Yeah, we had a word or two,' Reed murmured, as though talking to himself.

'You got a tough crust on you, feller. I knew you'd been tailin' us for a long time ... thought you'd given up. You goin' to shoot me here?'

Reed pulled out Hite's gun, took a deep breath and heard the roar of blood in his ears.

'My men, Sawyer,' Hite was saying again. 'Don't forget my men.'

Reed blinked hard, got his senses going again. 'You ain't got any men. Not any more.'

Hite shook his head slowly, as if in disbelief, but he didn't take his eyes from Reed's face. Then a thin smile touched his lips. 'You're lying, Sawyer, and you're not going to die because of me.'

Reed moved far too quick for either of the men to react. He switched the gun to his left hand, poled his right fist hard between Claye's eyes.

'Don't move,' he told Hite, as Claye went over backwards, crashing from his chair on to the floor.

'Knowing what I know, I'd say you've gone soft,' Hite said, looking down at Claye's unmoving body.

'No, I ain't gone soft,' Reed said, with a black look. 'Only this ain't the way I'd thought it out. I want me another time. Now you get to your feet.'

But Hite didn't move. 'If you caught up with this Packman, you must have got your hands on that land deed,' he suggested. 'And a most valuable document it's become.' Reed's hush seemed to satisfy him, and he smiled. 'Not killin' Claye right now, could be a big mistake. Don't go making another one: you and me can cut a deal.'

Reed pulled back his fist, stared into Hite's face. 'That deed weren't me an' Packman's only business, an' it ain't the reason he's dead. Now, what deal you talkin' about?' he asked menacingly.

Hite exhaled, let the breath whistle through his teeth. 'It was just an idea. Let's go.' He pushed himself up from the table, moved to the door that Reed indicated.

At the instigation of Reed's Colt, Hite crossed the darkened yard. He glanced towards the bunkhouse, wondered what Reed had done to Fijo and Mickens. Reed was wondering the same about Mickens, the man who'd gone to tend to the horses.

'What have you done to my men?' Hite asked, looking back over his shoulder.

'They'll live. One of 'em's got a sore head. Go on, keep movin'.'

Reed steered them wide around the hay barn, on to the stand of cottonwoods. In the darkness, Reed caught sight of his roan, then the Big Greasewood chestnut mare. 'Hold up,' he called.

Reed walked quickly over to his horse and mounted. He swung around on Hite. 'Listen,' he said. 'You know I'm a real mean son-of-a-bitch. Well, if you so much as break wind, I'll ride back.' Then he toed the stirrups and flicked the reins. As he moved through the trees, he heard Hite's calculated drawl.

'We'll meet again, cowboy.'

Reed knew that was true and wondered how long. He felt a stab of defeat as he kicked out from the deep darkness of the trees, headed east across the flats. Within minutes they'd be on his trail, and if Hite spun the Big Greasewood crew a line, there'd be a big pack of them. He swore long and profuse. His long journey down to the ranch with the chestnut mare had seemingly come to nothing.

As he rode, Reed pushed the last half-hour

through his mind. Hite had mentioned the land deed. That meant Claye must have told him. And as the two of them weren't killing each other when Reed had arrived, they'd obviously come to some sort of agreement. They'd run him down together, that was it. Reed slapped the reins, called for more effort from the roan.

In less than an hour of running, Reed realized he should have taken the chestnut mare. He'd pushed his roan at a savage pace when he'd gone after Packman, relentless before that. Now the horse's neck and shoulders were dropping, and it was frequently missing a stride. It was a fine mount, but one that was reaching the limit of its endurance.

He rode more easy, and after another few miles, he stopped on a rising slope of long grass. They both needed a few hours' rest, and Reed had to gather his thoughts, consider his next move. He quickly threw off the saddle and his traps, close-hobbled the roan. Very shortly there'd be a posse of men on his trail, and maybe Gilpin Boyle's coonhound. He could keep riding west, take the higher ground south of Fort Union. But that would surely kill the roan. And Catherine Gilkicker wanted her land deed back, and *he* wanted Athol Cade. Either of these things would hold him, even without his concern for Mercy Claye, or the unremitting anxiety he felt for his kid sister.

Reed squinted back at Big Greasewood's mighty acreage, distant and draped in moonlight. His prospect was to hole up and wait for Hite's men to quit their search – days for which he wasn't too well provisioned. He had another more thoughtful swear, remembered his pa once saying that everything came to those who waited. He sat with his chin on his knees, thought maybe he'd spot the first sign of his pursuers.

14

SQUARING THE ODDS

During the next few hours, Reed drifted towards sleep several times. But nervous anticipation kept him awake. At dawn's first light, he remained tired, and his muscles were cramped as he unhobbled the roan.

He held the horse to a controlled pace, and by mid-morning he was close to the timbered foothills of the Cristos. Soon he'd be deep within the sanctuary of the pine, but he knew that a good tracker or a hound would find him. He looked anxiously over his shoulder as he divested his chaqueta against the rising heat.

It was a half-hour later that he picked out the distant shimmering movements. They were the horsemen from Big Greasewood, and they were closing fast. But he held the pace, because the last thing he wanted to do was stove up the roan and put himself on foot.

Where land began to break into the trees, he took another rest, watched the tired horse pull at grass and high clover. The riders were nearer now. Reed was long-seen and they were coming for him, head on. He took another long look, saddled up and moved on. A shallow, tree-filled gully took him up, then shelved to the grassy ruts of an unused logging road. He crossed it, guessed that if he took its north trail, he'd end up somewhere near Elias Claye's lumber camp. Beyond the track, the land went immediately into a steeper climb. Then it was into the stands of dense, tall timber, and Reed allowed himself a breath at the cover it afforded.

For several more miles he rode through the trees, until moss-covered rocks and deep fissures surrounded him. There was a bubbling stream and Reed decided to haul in. He knew Hite's men must be almost on him, decided it was as good a place as any to make a last-ditch stand. Then through the aromas of fern and resin, he caught the unmistakable drift of wood smoke.

'Jesus, there's someone else,' he said, almost aloud. Hoping it was a trapper, he pulled his Colt and walked on slowly. He ducked the low branches, watched the roan's feet tread the soft, piny mulch. The smoke drifted in again, but this time stronger. Ahead of him, a knot of brome-grass ran to the bank of a stream. Beside it, a camp-fire made a light crackle as it burned unattended.

He pushed his Colt back into his holster and, holding the reins loose and high, he asked the roan to walk on. A fat-burned pan and a coffee jug had been set on the ground close by the fire.

'You're out there watchin',' Reed muttered, as he swung down from the saddle. 'Don't waste these fixin's on account o' me,' he called out, standing away from his horse. 'I ain't here to do harm.'

He turned slowly when he heard the soft rustle of duff behind him, breathed out when Cawden Fisher stepped from the cover of a bull pine. The youngster was smiling, slope-arming a Springfield rifle.

'You can't stay lonely too long up here,' Fisher said, walking to his fire. He laid his gun down and pulled his hand back into the sleeve of his short coat. Then he lifted the hot coffee jug away from the fire, pulled off the lid and offered it up. Reed nodded and moved to hunker beside the kid. Fisher poured him some coffee and Reed was suddenly aware of his craving for food and drink.

He coughed and spluttered. 'It's good to see you, kid. But I got a posse on my trail. They ain't exactly sworn in, an' they ain't interested in legal detail. So if there's a trail east out o' these trees, just tell me.'

Fisher unfolded a clasp-knife, eyed his frying pan. 'The only way out's the way you came in. Bet it's the long beard from Las Vegas you gone an' upset,' he said.

'Yeah, Shelby Hite. An' he's got riders.'

'How many?'

'Not sure. Could be a whole pack of 'em.'

'Hmm,' Fisher said, having a stab at the pan. 'Well, if they think they're takin' on one, two'll be a mighty surprise.'

'Seems like you're my guardian angel, kid. But this time you're well out of it. I'm gone by the time they come through here.'

'Relax,' Fisher said. 'I heard you comin' from the time you crossed the lumber trail. Sound carries up here to beat all hell. You'll hear 'em in plenty o' time. Why not eat somethin'?'

Reed looked uncertainly at the pan. He was worried at Fisher's cool, guessed it must be the value of youth. 'What *is* this?' he asked.

'Trappers call it slum-gullion. That's meat an' onions,' Fisher said, and handed over his knife with a chunk speared on the stubby blade.

Reed bit into the dark, unctuous meat. Fisher smiled indulgently, sat back on his haunches to build a cigarette. Reed decided to finish off the stew, mopped up the juices with a thick, doughy biscuit. He looked over at Fisher, saw the boy was watching him.

'It's sure peaceful up here,' he said.

'Yep. Gives you time to think ... set out your priorities,' Fisher replied with a curious wisdom.

'I guess you didn't need me bustin' in on you.'

Fisher's quick grin appeared. 'Hell, it don't matter. Someone had to eat that goddamn coon.' They both laughed, and Fisher relit his cigarette. 'I *was* getting bored, anyways.' He gave Reed a quizzical look then. 'I figured you and Hite had unfinished business. Didn't reckon on bein' in the middle again though. What's the set-up?'

'You sure got yourself a knot o' worms there. I'm real sorry about your sister,' Fisher responded, after Reed had told him best part of the story. 'An' like I said, I'm getting bored.'

'An' like *I* said,' Reed told him, quietly, 'if you could just point 'em in the wrong direction when they ride through, I'd be grateful.'

Fisher was already shaking his head. 'Nope. Don't reckon I can do that.'

'Look, kid, this is my fight. I don't want to blight all the thinkin' you been doin', but gettin' killed shouldn't be a great priority.'

Fisher flashed his grin again. 'I'm involved. Got that way when I stuck the end o' my gun into Mr Hite back there in the saloon.'

Reed saw Fisher give the 'that's the way it is' shrug of his shoulders, knew there was little he could do to make him think differently.

'If you've made up your mind,' he said, 'I've got a couple more reasons.'

'Yeah?' Fisher said, pulling a fir cone from the needles and bark around his feet.

'Yeah. Who else is goin' to help them two women?'

While he was thinking, Fisher tossed the cone into the fire, waited for it to flare alight. 'You talkin' about Miss Gilkicker, an' the Claye girl?'

'That's them. You reckon the odds are worth it?'

Fisher got to his feet, gave the brim of his hat a tug. 'You serious? With pretty kittens as prizes?' he laughed.

15

THE BODY BLOW

Reed and Fisher wedged themselves into deep, rocky fissures either side of the stream. Reed thumbed cartridges into the soft moss, made a neat row, convenient for a reload. As soon as they'd decided to make a stand, Reed was thinking on what came next.

'You ever shoot a man?' he asked of Fisher.

'No, not as such. Faced one or two down though.'

'Yeah, well, that ain't *quite* the same, kid. But all that's just about to change. Remember, group your shots. We want to pin 'em down.'

'What happens if they all come head on, tight out o' the trees?'

'That's different. You shoot to kill.'

An hour later, they saw the rising hawk before picking out the sound of the approaching riders. Reed held the barrel of his sister's rifle against the damp rock, bore down on the shadows across the break in the trees. Unsuspecting, it was Shelby Hite and one of his men who rode into view. Reed glanced at Fisher who nodded and held his fire.

Reed placed his shot between the front feet of Hite's mount. The big grey shied, but Hite held him in. Then Reed nodded, and Fisher fired into the ground beneath the other rider's horse. The bullet threw up shards of blowdown and the horse reared, its rider wrestling for control. Reed had pressed a fresh cartridge into the breech, but Hite was already turning his grey back into cover of the trees. The second rider had a nervous glance around him, frog-walked his horse after his boss.

A long minute passed before they heard Hite's strained voice. 'Sawyer?' he called out. 'Who you got there, Sawyer?'

'The Texas Rangers. An' they come fully tooled,' Reed replied.

Hite gave a edgy laugh. 'I'm thinkin' maybe you got that kid with you. The one rode in with Herran Tudor.'

'Oh him? Yeah, he's here as well.'

Fisher couldn't hold back his chuckle as they listened to Hite's blistering curses. 'Yep, I'm here,' Fisher said, then stood and fired three quick shots into the dark cover of the trees to emphasize it.

They settled for a long vigil then. An hour after sunset, the light gave way to flat, shadowless dark and still Hite made no move. Fisher hemmed and hahhed, stirred restlessly. 'What the hell's he waitin' for, Reed?' he asked.

'Full dark, same as us.'

'You got an idea for what happens then?'

'I'm still thinkin',' Reed said truthfully.

'Hey,' Hite shouted. The man was closer now, in tight to the nearest of the trees. 'Don't be a fool, kid. This ain't your business. Ride back to where you came from. You'll be safe enough.'

Fisher winked across at Reed. 'Yeah, sure,' he called back. 'An' you who paid to gun down an old man. I'm lackin' years, not wits, smock-face.'

This time it was Reed's turn to grin at Fisher's insouciance.

'I want the paper Sawyer's holdin'. That worth dyin' for?' Hite continued.

Fisher and Reed looked hard at each other. Whatever happened, they knew they wouldn't be allowed to ride out. Besides, Reed wasn't sure the whereabouts of Elias Claye and his ranch hands.

'You've had your warnin', Sawyer. You're goin' to find it's a long night.'

In the full dark, Reed climbed the rock fissure. He'd seen rising colour from a line of distant fires. They were spread across the back trail, would light the shadows of a trapped man's route to freedom.

'I've done thinkin', kid,' Reed said. 'We'll run at 'em . . . go like lard through a goose. We won't give 'em a chance to think.'

'When?'

'How about right now?'

For nearly fifteen minutes, Reed and Fisher worked at carefully saddling their horses. Reed noticed that Fisher was trembling, guessed it was tension, and sweat-chilled by the night.

'My guts is a mess, Reed,' Fisher said.

'Yeah, me too, kid. You just follow me through, you hear.'

Then they mounted and rode out, picked their way gently through the tall, dark bull pine. Reed hardly took his eyes off the fire line, listened for the slightest warning that they'd been seen.

He kept the roan at a steady, slow walk until they came to within fifty feet of the first fire glow. Two mackinaw-wrapped figures were snugged close, and a guard cradling a rifle sat against a tree bole. The brim of his slouch hat was pulled down and his head was drooped. To Reed, it didn't look like he was razor-sharp.

'No need for a trumpet,' he muttered, and turned to wave Fisher on. He dug his spurs and the roan leaped for the space around the fire, and the darkness beyond. Reed leaned into the charge, but chose the wrong side of the roan's neck. He felt the hammer blow in the middle of his back, heard the great crash of the guard's rifle.

Reed gasped, pulled himself back in the saddle. He knew the bullet was high and deep inside his shoulder. It was bad, but his hands retained their grip. From behind, Fisher's gun blasted twice. and yells from the camp shattered the night. Someone screamed and Fisher was suddenly by his side. Together, they raced deep into the trees, away from the confusion and the deadly fire traps.

A half-hour later, they were huddled beneath the slant of a rocky outcrop. They were on the timberline, where pine met the lower slopes of the grass land. There was still enough moon for Fisher to see the dark shine between Reed's shoulders.

'This sure is sticky, Reed. You sure you ain't full o' molasses?' Fisher said, looking at his blood-wet fingers. 'I'd better get some rock moss to stuff in the hole. You'll be empty soon.'

Reed was sitting with his forehead pressed hard against his knees. He was in trouble now, almost delirious, fighting off black pulses of pain that exploded across his body.

'I can't do much, an' we can't stay here, Reed,' Fisher was saying. 'We got to find us a safe place before daylight.'

'We can hold 'em off,' Reed coughed up painfully.

'What for? So's you can let 'em see you die? You don't want the sepsis. You need some physic an' a doc to sew you up.'

'Back to Las Vegas then, eh, kid? Looks like you're the leader o' the gang now.'

'Yeah, looks like it,' Fisher agreed anxiously. 'But it's some way. Reckon you can make it?'

'I can, if you hog me to the saddle. Don't run us though – the roan's a heck more'n winded.'

Fisher's face showed his concern. 'We still got trouble, then,' he said. 'They'll pick up our trail at first light, an' pound leather.'

'If we beat 'em into town, there's someplace you can lay me up. Only. . . .' Reeds eyes closed and his words faded with a grimace.

16

THE POSSUM PLAY

Catherine Gilkicker drew a shawl around her shoulders. She looked at the hardly touched food in front of her, pushed the plate away irritably. She was tired out, and her head ached dully from lack of sleep.

The story of Mina getting shot by Benton Mole had been all over town the following morning. Cassie shivered as she remembered the look on Reed Sawyer's face when he'd left her house to go after Mole. And now she knew it was Reed, not the lawyer, who engaged her concern. The shooting had to be paid for, but she didn't want the blood to be on Reed's hands.

By a twist of fate, it was then that the back door to Cassie's house took a sudden thump. She gasped, got to her feet at the second hammered blow of a fist. She moved quickly and pulled the bolt, stood back as the door swung open.

Reed's head was hanging into his chest, and his body was slumped heavily against Cawden Fisher.

'You Miss Gilkicker?' Fisher asked, at the same time pushing on into the room. He staggered, nearly fell with the unbalanced weight of Reed. They were both bearded and dust-grimed, and Reed's clothes were dark stained. Cassie felt a wave of sickness at the raw smell that pervaded her house, the cloy of sweat and Reed's blood.

'Where to, ma'am?' Fisher was almost shouting.

'Put him in my room. Quick, bring him through.'

Cassie opened a door off the parlour and pointed to the neatly made cot. Fisher stumbled forward, eased Reed out of his coat and laid him face down on a clean sheet. Cassie gently turned his head on the pillow as Fisher took a step back.

'Reed said somethin' about his sister bein' here,' he said.

'Yes, she was. The doctor's wife's got a sick-room at the other end of town. Now she's there, and just as well.'

'Is the doc there too?' Fisher asked eagerly.

'I doubt it. Mina's recovering well enough. Tell me how this happened.'

Fisher removed his hat, dragged his sleeve across his mouth. He talked quickly, and Cassie studied his young face, saw the strain of someone who'd been dragged quickly through the growing years.

'I didn't know all of that, it's hard to believe. I

don't know your name,' she said kindly.

'It's Cawden Fisher, ma'am.'

'Well, Cawden, you say Shelby Hite's on his way here?'

'Yes, ma'am. We had a good few hours on 'em out of the foothills. But with Reed the way he is though, we lost a lot o' that. Hite's got a tracker who'll cut our trail before first light. He'd've seen us makin' for town an' come on fast. They'll be real close now. They don't know where we're laid up though, ma'am. Our mounts are out back; you can't see 'em from the road.'

'Oh, Hite will guess,' Cassie said. 'You said that Reed's got my deed, and that Hite's after it?'

'That's right, ma'am. Well, it's what Reed said.' Fisher drew the paper from Reed's coat and handed it to Cassie.

With one hand, Cassie turned back a fold. She met Fisher's reserved look. 'Yes, that's it,' she said, and laid it on the cotside table.

'I sure hope it was worth it,' Fisher said more openly.

'Nearly at the cost of a life, you mean?'

'Reed's life, ma'am.'

'Yes. I'm sorry. What do you propose we do now then, to save him?'

'I thought that out,' Fisher said 'But the doctor's goin' to have to wait. That'll only bring attention here. I can lead Hite away with a fresh horse. I'll run ours to the livery, rent me a runner. When Hite rides in, I'll let him see my dust. With luck, he'll reckon it's me that's got that land paper. He'll try to ride me down again.'

'And if he doesn't?'

'I don't rightly know, ma'am. That's somethin' I'm goin' to leave you with. If they don't follow me though, I'll know soon enough. If they get to you here, you stall 'em for as long as it takes . . . until I get back.'

Cassie nodded. 'I'll think of something. Now you better hurry, Cawden. God speed.'

As soon as Fisher had gone, Cassie went to tend to Reed. She knelt beside the bed and listened to his breathing, laid her fingers across his sallow, sticky forehead. 'I'm so sorry,' she said, her heart pounding. 'It's a curious fortune that we share.' She knew he needed medical attention, but she couldn't risk going for the doctor. That could only happen when Shelby Hite had been and gone.

Cassie prepared a basin of hot water, and with a clean cloth, soaked, then teased away the bloody tatters that had been Fisher's field-dressing. She was startled by the fresh blood that flowed from the wound, but she made a compress and wadded it firmly around his chest. As she tied off the ends of the bandaging, she heard the clamour she'd been expecting from the street outside.

She closed her eyes, made the fleetest prayer whilst shoving the basin and bloodstained cloths under the cot. She draped a flowered dress across Reed's legs, quickly pulled some undergarments from a drawer and placed them conspicuously on top. Then she lifted the sheet to cover Reed's face, covered it with a chemise. It was all she could think of and hoped it was enough for the deception.

Then she went from the room back to the parlour and opened the front door. She stepped on to the porch, looked along the dusty street where Shelby Hite and his men had pulled up. They were obviously confused, were turning their horses, uncertain of a route to take.

Hite saw her watching and hesitated a moment before shouting his frustration.

'Fijo, you go an' talk to Miss Gilkicker, like I said. Take Juice and have a good look around. I'll go after the kid. If you don't find what we're lookin' for, follow us.'

Cassie slammed her door closed. She bit her lip and looked around the parlour, hurried in to the bedroom. She sat at the end of the cot thinking. She knew the man Fijo by sight. He'd passed her in the street, on one occasion had acknowledged her, she remembered. He was the one to use, she decided.

A moment later, she heard the Chicano rapping his knuckles on the door. She rose, quickly, as if irritated, and went to answer it. Fijo was standing there with his hat in his hand. Beside him was Juice Mickens, who returned her glare with a smirk.

'Yes, like most of the town, I heard,' Cassie got in first. 'Although I can't begin to think what it is you're looking for.'

'We're lookin' for someone, ma'am. We think he might've come here. We got to see inside your house.'

'That sounds like the sort of thing I'd know,

don't you think . . . a man in my house?' Cassie snapped angrily.

'Yes, ma'am,' Fijo agreed calmly.

Cassie opened the door wider, stood back as the men entered. 'Who is this man?' she asked.

'Reed Sawyer,' Mickens said.

'Reed Sawyer? And you think he's here, with me?' Cassie gasped with suitable astonishment.

Mickens sniggered and said something under his breath. Fijo's elbow jabbed into his stomach and he wheezed at the pain.

'Shut your face,' Fijo snarled, 'an' take off your hat.'

Fijo stepped uneasily from the parlour to the kitchen and Mickens followed him sullenly. At the doorway of Cassie's bedroom, the two men stopped.

Cassie stepped in front of Mickens, beside Fijo. The muscles around her mouth twitched and her heart leapt when she saw she hadn't moved the land deed from the table beside the cot. Rigid with apprehension, she stood watching Fijo look around the room, saw his eyes on the bundle that was Reed Sawyer.

'Oh, that . . . that's my . . . my wash, my underlinen. I'm sorry . . . I didn't think . . . wasn't expecting. . . .' She flustered with what she hoped passed for embarrassment.

It had the desired unsettling effect on Fijo and he coughed, turned his attention to the parlour.

'Ma'am, this Sawyer killed Lawyer Mole. So we got to see what we got to see. An' we know you know him . . . know both of 'em in fact. We put a bullet in Sawyer, and he'll be lookin' for someplace to lick his wounds, so to speak.'

'And you think he'd choose my home to do *that*?' Cassie sounded off her effrontery. 'What authority have you got to be here?' she demanded. She tried to hide her shock at the news of Benton Mole's death, her own culpability.

'We're a company o' men been hired to find him, an' you're sayin' you ain't seen him. Is that it, ma'am?'

'Yes, that's precisely it,' Cassie lied. 'It's true, I did . . . do know them. In fact Mr Sawyer was in my employ for a short while. But that was the limit of our relationship, and I don't take kindly to your intrusion into my home.'

Taken in by the force of Cassie's lies, Fijo pulled on his hat. 'Sorry, ma'am,' he said, somewhat contritely. 'Just doin' what I get paid for. No lastin' harm done, I hope. Let's go, Juice.'

Cassie pushed the door to, leaned her back against it, as the two men stepped away from her porch. She took a deep breath to try and control her trembling, then she went into her bedroom. removed her strewn clothing from the cot and pulled back the sheet. Reed had not moved; he was very still, but breathing more easily. She eased down the sheet a little more, saw the blood had begun to seep through the wound dressing. What she didn't notice was that Reed's hand had been gripping his Colt. His arm was bent, the gun tucked deep into his midriff.

'Now, I can get the doc.' she said, hoping Reed could hear. 'I know what you've still got to do.'

17

LAYING THE LAND

Troubled, Elias Claye stood looking out from the wide veranda of Big Greasewood's main house. With regard to his cousin, Mercy, he'd led Shelby Hite to suppose the worst for her. Now he feared the implication of that committal. Athol Cade, the rebel guerrilla, the bushwhacker would have ruthlessly crushed any such aggravation. But although young Mercy had become the hurdle to his greed, it was five years since he'd worn the red cockade. He was no longer the man to murder his uncle's daughter in cold blood. The devil was driving though, and he had to find a way.

Before Hite had left to go after Reed Sawyer, Fijo and Juice Mickens had ordered the Big Greasewood cowboys off the ranch. The man they called Rib had his hand shattered when Fijo loosed off a shot to contain him in the bunkhouse. Later, Claye had given the big man a half-bottle of bourbon, told him to lie up and he'd get him the doctor from town.

Elias Claye wasn't worried about the men returning. They were working cowhands, had no wish to get involved with Hite's paid gunmen. Loyalty to Vernon Claye might have drawn a fight from them, but now there was a new boss. Gilpin Boyle wasn't normally a man to run, but he saw no percentage in staying, and with his coonhound, took the trail towards Tucumcari. He'd been a long-time foreman, and loyal to Big Greasewood, but Claye didn't reckon he'd be coming back.

That left Reed Sawyer and Shelby Hite, who, Claye hoped, would be killing each other. He shuddered at the memory of Reed Sawyer's face, knew that next time, there'd be no reprieve. As for his pact with Hite, it was about as honourable as a white-man's tongue to an Apache. Hite possessed a ruthless greed to match his own, but the real danger was that it was only Mercy and himself who knew how his uncle had died.

Claye thought on the one-way ticket. He didn't need Hite, but Hite needed him. But once rid of Hite, he had to find the land deed and destroy it, together with that carried by Catherine Gilkicker. Only then would he be more secure. It was a day and a half since Hite had pursued Reed Sawyer north from Big Greasewood, so the deed might already be in Hite's possession. Claye shook the present reality, the problem of young Mercy back into his head.

He stepped down from the veranda, let his hand

idly push at the swing that hung from the cottonwood. As he walked across the yard to the bunkhouse, the early eastern light warmed his back.

Rib didn't look so big or meaty now. He was lying on his bunk, his upper body pasty and glistening with sweat. His right arm was held by a loose sling, and the fingers were wrapped in bloody bandaging; a revolver lay on the rumpled bed sheet. The man watched bad-temperedly as Claye approached him.

'They left you a gun then? Wonder what they thought you'd need it for?' Claye said.

Rib didn't respond to the sarcasm. 'Goddamn it,' he hissed, 'you promised me a doctor, not a rawly kid. She's got as much feelin' as a blackthorn.'

And you're just as spiky, Claye thought. But he didn't agree openly, considered that Rib might have something he could go along with.

'She sure ain't got the angel's touch,' he suggested, then started in on his plan. 'There's hospitals up north, that'll fix that busted hand for you. Send you packin' as good as new.'

'Yeah? An' at a dollar a day, you think I got that sort o' stash?' Rib sneered painfully.

'No. But I have. I'll pay for the surgery an' give you a stake,' Claye nodded encouragingly.

'The hell you will. Who do I have to kill?'

Claye pulled a wad of cash from his pocket, ten-dollar bills that he'd taken from his uncle's key safe. 'I'm not sayin' a name. You work it out.'

Rib's eyes rolled around while he had thoughtful moment, then his jaw dropped. 'Jeeesus,' he wheezed, 'that's a real bad business.'

Claye lifted his boot on to the bunk, placed it across the barrel of Rib's Colt. 'With that mess of a hand, you're down to the blanket, now, Rib,' he said, his voice low and sinister. 'But I'm offerin' you three years' pay in one go. Weigh it up. An' remember, out here, death by misadventure don't even get recorded.'

Rib stared at him silently for a while. 'Death by misadventure,' he repeated, as the thought of a thousand dollars sank in.

Claye was back to standing out front of the main house. He swiped at an angry wasp, as he watched Mercy turn the buggy on to the wagon road.

Rib had blamed his behaviour on the pain, the effect of too much unused-to bourbon. In what appeared to be deep regret, he'd persuaded Mercy to take him into town to see the doctor. It was getting away from the ranch, more than her compassionate nature, that obliged her to make the journey.

Claye knew that sooner or later, Rib would get roostered, and probably in Shelby Hite's saloon. The man would mouth on about how he'd been hired to get rid of Mercy Claye . . . paid by the girl's own cousin.

But it wasn't going to happen because he'd only paid Rib $250. To get the rest of the money there'd be no time for Rib to hang around. He'd have to return to Big Greasewood. Then, Claye would arrange for him to join his old employer.

There weren't too many people who would notice the absence of Rib, not too many who actually knew his second name. The man had value though. He'd be clearing the decks, leaving Elias Claye the only claimant to Big Greasewood.

Claye turned his thoughts to Shelby Hite. He made up his mind that if the saloon keeper hadn't returned by dusk, he'd ride into Las Vegas. He'd seek to surprise him there, hoped the man's gunnies had been paid, that they wouldn't press for a fight that didn't concern them.

Claye inspected the end of a new cigar, then turned on his heel. He thought maybe he'd walk around the house and make an appraisal, take full stock.

18

THE EVIL EYE

Cawden Fisher had less than a ten-minute lead on Shelby Hite when he dug spurs from Las Vegas. But he was astride a fresh livery mount, would outdistance the pursuers.

He paced them at first, stayed on open ground to lure them into the chase. He guessed one of the two would be Shelby Hite, the others should still be looking through Catherine Gilkicker's rooms. He rode uneasy though, because he knew that Hite wouldn't be easily fooled.

To the north-west, he saw the rising timberline of the Cristos and, knowing that country, he veered there in an all-out run. The livery horse fought the bit, but it was what he wanted, a rangy and powerful mare. After a half-hour ride, he headed up one of the rising trails that brought him to within a few hundred yards of the timber, close to the old logging track. He pulled in to take a breather, look to his backtrail.

Now Fisher spotted four horsemen. He knew that would be the two from town joining with Hite and the other one. He watched as they formed a line, as they commenced their ride towards the timberline. Fisher smiled. They hadn't got their hands on Catherine Gilkicker's land deed, hadn't found Reed.

He went into the trees and immediately swung north, then down the long sloping trail to where he estimated he'd cut the wagon road to Big Greasewood's main house. It was only a mile from where he'd ridden the previous night, where he'd tied Reed to the saddle of his roan, ridden down into Las Vegas. Fisher recalled the words Reed repeated as he slumped in and out of consciousness. 'You get to Mercy Claye, kid. She needs help.'

Fisher had seen the girl only the one brief time. It was the day that Reed had shot Herran Tudor to save her father. He'd admired her tallness and red hair, put her down as someone not too far off his own age.

Another hour's hard riding, and Fisher met up with the Big Greasewood wagon road, gave the mare an added heel kick. He knew he was beyond Segundo Flat, couldn't be more than five miles from the house. But Elias Claye had been planning his move for many hours, and Fisher was suddenly fearful of being too late.

Then, up ahead, around a long bend and through the screen of roadside willow, he saw the buggy. There were two people, and it turned away from the road at a curious angle. He held the mare in for a while, then trotted it forward to the spot where the buggy had gone into the willow and cottonwood. Off to his left, Fisher could hear the gurgle of water and he rode forward cautiously. He brushed aside the low hanging branches until he saw the sheen of wet moss and fern ahead of him. Where the stream coursed out of a rocky fissure it was broad and deep enough to prevent the crossing of a light vehicle.

He could see a short way downstream, saw the wheel ruts in the soft ground where the buggy had turned away. He dismounted and led the mare quietly forward a few paces, held up at the sound of voices ahead. It was a girl speaking, and it came from a willow brake that was edging the stream.

There was a high cutbank, and Fisher loose-hitched the mare before sliding down to the chill water. The high, root-woven bank would screen him from above and he drew his Colt, moved stealthily along the stream bed. Beneath the overhang of the trees he hunkered down, listened to the imploring of Mercy Claye.

'Please. In two days I can be in Albuquerque. There's trains west to Kansas City . . . St Louis even. Elias will never know the difference. I can get money to make good what he promised you. Think, Rib. Can you trust a man who wants to murder his own kin?'

The last of the bourbon that Rib had consumed was doing its work. 'You'll go blabber,' he slurred.

'No. I want to stay alive too,' she said, desperately. 'I just want to get away. I swear.'

'Yeah? Well, maybe I got my own reasons for bringin' you out here, you little mockey,' the man now threatened.

Fisher relaxed his shoulders, did some fast, shallow breathing. Most parts of him were sweating at the thought of what he had to do. He'd only get one shot, and it would have to be accurate once he raised himself above the bank. He wanted to get close, beneath Rib who'd be sitting nearest. He moved carefully, held his breath until he was practically underneath and sideways on to Rib's head and shoulders.

'It's goin' to look like the horse got spooked. Yeah, you got thrown from your seat . . . dragged an' banged your pretty li'l head . . . ended up rat-drowned,' Rib said, trying to put together a new plan.

Fisher straightened fast. He shifted the weight of one foot, raised the other and dug it into the low bank. But the moist earth gave way and he lost his balance, staggered backwards into the water. His foot slipped on loose pebbles and the water swirled strongly around his legs. He threw out an arm and went down, couldn't help the splashing.

Rib half stood in the buggy. He swung around tightly, turned his revolver towards the sound below him. But he wasn't set right. With his busted hand, he couldn't steady himself and his nerves were stretched.

Fisher went under as Rib's gun roared. He kept his gun hand extended, didn't see or hear the bullet as it plunged into the water alongside his submerged head. He pushed himself up on to his knees, with one hand brushed at the chill water that flowed across his face.

As Rib cursed, tried again to stand for a better view of Fisher, Mercy jumped from the rig. The vehicle swayed, and for a moment, Rib's mean and pained features appeared above the top of the bank.

Fisher saw him and was ready. He blew a gobbet of water from his lips as he brought Rib's head into his gun sight. 'Bastard,' he muttered, and pulled the trigger.

Rib's head jerked back and his body went lifeless. It crashed across a back wheel of the buggy, then fell heavily to the ground. Fisher scrambled to his feet, ramming his gun back into its holster. He pulled his hat from a root tangle and again went for the cutbank. Scrambling and then half falling, he made it, settled on his knees, to gape at the dead man who lay less than a dozen feet away.

Rib was on his back. Fisher's bullet had taken him somewhere between his mouth and the bridge of his nose. Fisher felt his stomach heave as he looked to where Mercy stood, terrified. He leaned down, pulled at Rib's coat until the man's bloody mess of a face was turned in to the ground.

'I reckon you're indebted to *me* now, Miss Claye,' he said, recalling what she'd once told Reed.

'I know,' Mercy said, almost inaudibly. 'Do you think I've brought an evil eye to this place?'

'If you have, it ain't on those who matter,' he told her, shaking his head, and thinking that maybe he'd won the first kitten. He went for his best grin, made it fleeting because his next concern was the whereabouts of Shelby Hite and his men.

19

VENGEFUL THOUGHTS

Reed's face had paled, and the small scars were etched clearer. But he was tough enough, only needed some sleep and rest for the healing to begin.

There'd been trauma, real bad moments while the doctor sought the bullet that was embedded deep in his shoulder. Then, he went off into the black void, slept soundly again for another few hours.

It was full dark when he regained consciousness. He was lying on his side, saw yellow light from beneath the bedroom door. In the parlour, he could hear the doctor saying something to Cassie.

'Hello?' he called, his voice parched and grated.

Cassie opened the door, walked quickly to the cot. In the light from the parlour, she could see

Reed's straggling fair hair, the gleam of his eyes as he looked up at her.

'That was the doc,' she said. 'He called in again to check on you, and bring some laudanum. The wound was a bad one, but it's clean, and there shouldn't be too much muscle damage. You're still running a fever though. You've got to rest up some more; you've been real lucky.'

'Lucky, yeah,' he rasped, moved by the acute pain of astonishment 'Where's Mina? And what's happened to the kid?'

'Your sister's almost back on her feet. Cawden's left town, though.'

'Left town? Where's he gone?'

'I'm not sure. But he's taken Shelby Hite with him. It's what he meant to do. He said he'll be back, tonight. I know he isn't, not yet anyway, but nor's Hite.'

'Goddamn kid's playin' hare'n hounds,' Reed groaned, and dropped his head back against the pillow, wondered if he was in the right place. 'You know I caught up with him, don't you? The man you know as Benton Mole.'

'Yes, I know,' Cassie said in a frail voice. 'And I know what your *real* reason was.'

Reed rolled his eyes back up to Cassie again, for the moment couldn't think of what to say.

'There was nothing more than a casual friendship between Benton – whatever his name was – and me. He wanted more than I was prepared to give. He told me that—' Cassie began to explain.

But Reed didn't want to hear it. 'So you know

why I went after him, why he shot Mina?' he cut in.

'Yes. Cawden told me. I'm so sorry, Reed. What happened all those years ago. I was thinking it was all about that stupid Castanar land deed.'

Reed grimaced, raised himself on to an elbow. 'It ain't stupid, Cassie, an' you weren't to know. I ain't finished either. Riddin' myself o' Packman weren't quite enough.'

Cassie lightly touched Reed's arm. 'You've got medicine for what troubles you now, Reed. There's none for hate,' she said tellingly.

'Sorry, Cassie. It's *revenge*, not hate. But Captain Athol Cade ain't livin' on the difference. Not after what he did to my folk . . . me an' Mina's folk.'

Cassie knelt beside the cot. 'Let it be, Reed. Let the law have him,' she asked.

Reed knew that if it hadn't been for Cassie, he'd more than likely be dead. And she'd got Mina's blood on her sheets, too. He didn't want to upset her more than he had to, more than she already was. 'This ain't your business, Cassie. You don't know what you're askin'.'

'I think I do. It was *me* who brought them all down on top of you. It was through me that you were forced to kill a man, almost getting yourself killed. And it's because of me that young Cawden's run off to God knows where. So, yes Reed, I do think I know what I'm asking.'

Reed moved his arm, let his fingers touch Cassie's hand. 'Oh well, if you put it like that,' he grinned with feigned submission. He had been thinking of Cawden Fisher, knew that if the kid had got away from Hite, he'd have ridden for Big Greasewood. He'd have gone to help Mercy Claye as Reed had asked him to. And now they were all in danger.

'Hite's goin' to come back,' he said.

'How do you know?'

'Because he'll work it out. You won't bluff him like you did the henchmen. We'll have to get out.' With Cassie's hesitant support, Reed moved up to a sitting position. Jaw clenched against the bitter pain, he swung his legs to the floor. He drew air noisily between his teeth and hauled himself to his feet, took one lumbering step forward.

'Let go,' he rasped, setting his weight. Cursing and swearing under his breath at the effort needed, he made his way from the bedroom into the kitchen. Cassie lit a hanging lamp above the table, and Reed pulled open a cupboard, had a look at the pantry shelves.

'Pack up some o' this food, an' some blankets,' he said. 'I'll go get the horses. An' don't forget that deed,' he smiled. 'You know, the stupid one you owe me fifty dollars for.'

Cassie smiled back. 'Maybe we should leave it for Hite.'

'It'll make no difference, Cassie. He'll be fully loco'd by now. Nothin' less than our lives is goin' to satisfy him.'

'How are you going to make it to the stable?' Cassie stepped closer, looked worriedly at Reed's face.

'I'll make it,' he said more strongly. 'It's just a

case o' gettin' one foot in front of another ... keepin' it goin'.' He demonstrated the movement, overcooked it and almost lost his balance. Cassie held on to him and for a moment they swayed together.

'Sorry,' he mumbled, and pushed his lips into the side of her neck. Then he moved round and kissed her properly. There was no resistance. He thought it must be the shock, and he moved away to apologize again.

'I was tryin' to go around you. Got my face in the way. Weren't my fault,' he explained.

'I'm sorry too. I just wasn't quick enough to get out of the way,' Cassie replied.

'Yeah, well, I'll be back as fast as I can,' he said, with a gruffness in his throat. 'You get that stuff bagged an' ready.'

20

TWO DOWN

Reed moved stealthily along the street's boardwalk. Where possible, he edged in close to the buildings, where not, he didn't remain too long in the open. Every so often he stopped, waited for the pains to ebb before continuing. Stepping up and down from the boardwalks, he swallowed hard, groaned inwardly at the surges of nausea as he kept his eyes on the near-deserted street. Against the night-time chill, his old chaqueta wore heavy across his shoulders. He had one Colt tucked into his pants, the other he carried beneath a fold of the coat.

He reached the livery and turned into the yard. Beside the sconced lamp, he waited for a moment, considered calling for the hostler. He thought better of it when he heard the sound of horsemen riding upstreet from the opposite end of town.

There was five of them riding abreast, and Reed

went for the interior of the stable. His heart was racing, filling his chest with hammer blows, but now there was nowhere else for him to go. Shelby Hite was back in town and headed straight for the yard.

Reed edged into a stall that was stacked high with damp, soiled straw, shuddered at the dark scuttling of a rat across his feet. With his back pressed against the slimed palings, he eased the action of his gun as he slid down a way. He couldn't move his face any nearer to the fetid pile of waste, crouched motionless and scarcely breathing as the riders pulled in to the yard.

Shelby Hite led them in. They weren't within Reed's line of sight, but he heard the snort of the mounts, the snap and creak of leather as the men dismounted. Hite shouted for Levy, the hostler, cursed him for not being around. The men sounded tired, moaned at their futile hard riding.

'Goddamn jasper's probably still here. I told you Fijo didn't make any real kind o' search,' rasped Juice Mickens. 'He went soft on the girl.'

'Yes, that's what I've been thinking must've happened,' Hite murmured. 'I think we paid the price for your gallantry, friend,' he called out to Fijo. 'Let's now go an' do it my way. Pink, you take care of the horses. Meet us down the street aways.'

Reed could just see four of the men as they walked past the open door of the livery. Levy still hadn't made an appearance and Reed watched and waited as the man called Pink walked the horses into the stable, tied them into the running rail.

He twisted the Colt around, cradled the frame in his palm. He slipped the fingers of his other hand through a split paling, pulled himself from the stall.

He gasped at the fresh strike of pain that ran through his chest, then again as he shrugged off his jacket.

He knew he couldn't get back to Cassie's house before Hite and his men got there. He'd have to take on all five of them near enough to where he was standing. In one of the shortest moments of thought, he recalled a newspaper headline when a notorious gunman had been shot down in Denver. An awestruck cub reporter had asked how he'd been able to shoot so many men. 'Mostly, I surprised 'em,' the man had answered, and then died.

'Wisecracker,' Reed muttered, to the disadvantage of the man who was hitching the horses.

A night breeze was blowing the flame from the lamp around, and its light flickered across Reed's face as he came forward. Pink turned, but couldn't do much. Reed slammed the frame of his Colt into the side of the man's surprised face.

As Pink went down, Reed looked along the street. He saw the backs of the four men walking towards Hite's Saloon, the other end of town and Cassie Gilkicker's house. One of the men wore a bleached slouch hat. He was dragging his foot, and his left arm was hanging limp. Reed wondered if he was the night guard who'd shot him, the one who'd caught a bullet or two from young Fisher.

With a gut feeling, the man turned around, saw Reed gasping in agony from the blow he'd just effected. He yelled an instinctive warning and the others halted. Then they backed off, spreading at the same time. From sixty feet, Hite plucked the slim cigarillo from between his teeth, hurled it disgustedly to the ground.

'Goddamn you, Sawyer. You sure are the most interfering son-of-a-bitch,' he snarled. 'I can pay you a small fortune *not* to die. What is it with you?'

'I was wonderin' the same about you, Hite,' Reed shouted back. 'It's Elias Claye I'm lookin' for. Tell me where he is, an' then go back to saloon-keepin'. Some of us get to live that way.'

'I can't do that, Sawyer. There's too much at stake now.'

Reed worked up some dry spit, wondered how anyone could endure such pain and still carry on. Perhaps that can be *my* surprise though, he told himself. Then he shrugged, smiled compliantly and swung up his Colt.

Hite had simultaneously guessed at Reed's play, and thrown himself sideways. He hit the ground as Reed's gun roared, heard the crash of a window shattering, his men cursing, throwing themselves for cover.

As Reed stepped back into the stable, he realized that he didn't feel pain any more, wondered if it was a bad sign. Then he saw Hite get to his feet, run crouched and desperate for the cover of a chocked-up wagon across the street. Hite made it as Reed fired again, ducked as the bullet whined off a steel-rimmed wheel.

Fijo was standing just inside the open doorway of a streetside building, firing calmly back to where Reed sought his cover. The already wounded man limped into a narrow passageway alongside. But Juice Mickens was standing his ground, was pumping rifle bullets through the doorway, up into the rafters of the stable. Reed hunkered down, pressed his back to the inside of the door frame. He felt the cold sweat through his shirt as bullets ploughed up the acrid dust of the dirt floor, as straw and grain fell from the hay loft above him. Then he heard Hite shout at Mickens to get off the street. It was an opportunity, and Reed waited for a moment before twisting low around the door post. Mickens was still under the influence of Hite's orders, and Reed took two quick shots. The man who worked for the price of a drink, was running towards the dark cover of the passageway, and he faltered as a bullet took him in the side. He stumbled on, pitched into a hitching rail. But he was already a dead weight and the poles cracked and crashed beneath him.

Hite, Fijo and the wounded man immediately opened up a barrage of gunfire. Reed kicked himself further into the barn, pulled his second Colt as the tethered horses began their startled whinnyng and stomping. He got to his feet and backed off, stared at the doorway and frame that was fast turning to matchwood.

'Hold your fire,' Fijo yelled. 'That must've slowed him down some.'

In the following moments of silence, Reed held back in the deep darkness, moved to get an angled view of the street outside. He saw Fijo, couldn't fire because he was a sitting duck for bullets fired through the open doors. Then he saw Hite waving for Fijo to go round the back of the barn. Reed stepped over the still unconscious Pink, moved back against a side wall to think. He knew his sister wasn't too far away, had a second of wondering what she'd make of the gunfire. Then he heard the footsteps pounding on a boardwalk, guessed the wounded man had left the passageway and was closing on the barn.

He was clean out of surprises, could only wait for Hite and his men to burst in on him. Through chinks in the clapboarding, he thought he saw a shadow moving along the side of the barn. He held out his two guns and fired, groaned as the agony racked his body once again.

He listened to the echoes of his gunfire, shook his head in confusion, when he realized the sounds were from outside of the barn, from somewhere close along the street.

Then Fijo was back in the main street again. He was obviously hit, couldn't elevate his gun arm to bear on whoever it was had joined the fight. Reed reeled back to the doorway, saw the Chicano kneeling, using both hands for a final shot. The unseen gunman fired again, and Fijo jerked, folded into the grey dirt of the street.

From the dark maw of the passageway, Cawden Fisher spurred his horse forward. He looked toward the barn, then quickly up and down the street, wondered about the two other men who were still menacing Reed Sawyer.

21

THREE TO GO

Shelby Hite shouted his wrath at the sight of Fijo falling, and stepped out from behind the shelter of the wagon. But Reed didn't want Cawden Fisher to deal with Hite. He began firing, used up the last two shots of one gun, took over with the other, as he too moved from his cover.

When Reed saw Hite facing the livery stable, throwing gunshots with an irrational defiance, he wondered why the borderline fight for Big Greasewood was worth dying for. But he knew he'd never find out, let alone ask the question, and he pulled the trigger again.

Hite dropped his gun and clutched his stomach. Then, as if thinking the same thing as Reed, he looked towards his saloon, grimaced as his legs gave way. He went down slowly with his back rubbed against the wagon wheel, closed his eyes as if surrendering to fatigue.

Reed heard a sound from back in the barn. He held up his hand to Fisher to stop him making another kill, continued his slow walk towards Hite. He hunkered down and looked into the dying man's eyes. 'You'da done the same to me,' he said. 'Now tell me where Claye is?'

The shadow of a sneer flicked across Hite's face. 'He's probably right behind you,' were his last words.

Reed grunted, moved aside the man's long wispy beard, pushed his hand under his coat and withdrew the disputed land deed. 'This ain't worth a plugged nickel to *you* any more,' he said quietly. He pushed it into his pocket and, shaking with full-size pain, he raised himself, turned to face Cawden Fisher.

'Well, if it ain't that guardian angel o' mine,' he growled.

Fisher tugged at the brim of his hat, nodded and sheathed his gun. 'Like I was tellin' you before,' he said, 'I reckon I got them priorities sorted.'

Reed saw Fisher suddenly look back towards the barn. It was the horse minder, Pink, and he was glaring defiantly. The man was holding the side of his face, and he walked unsteadily. He cast a quick glance over at Juice Mickens, then down at Hite.

'You kill 'em both?' he asked of Reed.

'Yeah. Either of 'em mean much to you?'

'No. You goin' to do for me?' the man asked, without much apparent concern.

'Don't reckon I could, even if I wanted to, which

I don't,' Reed told him. 'You go pick yourself the best o' them mounts an' ride on.' Reed's last few words were slurred to indistinction, but the man got the drift after looking up at Fisher.

'Look who's comin', Reed,' Fisher said, at the jounce of an approaching buggy.

Wondering how anyone so wounded and pained could still stand, Reed stared along the darkness of the street. He recognized the driver as Mercy Claye, watched as Fisher rode alongside and reached down for the mare's bridle. In the thin, wavering light, Reed saw the girl's worried features, her weariness. But she was unhurt, and the relief helped him.

For another couple of minutes he listened to Fisher's story, was distracted by one or two townsfolk, who'd started to mill around.

'No sign o' Claye, though,' Fisher said, peering anxiously into Reed's face. 'How you gettin' back to Miss Gilkickers?'

'Walkin'. Be interestin' to see how far I can get.'

Within a dozen laboured paces, Reed felt the core of his strength ebbing away. His shirt was clinging to his back, but not through sweat. It was the bullet wound that had opened, new blood that was spreading.

Goddamn hard way to earn me fifty dollars, he thought, as with a gun in each hand, he went doggedly on, up the street. He wanted away from Mercy Claye, because he couldn't fashion a way of telling her that he was still looking to kill her cousin. And that was when he realized what Hite had meant about the same man's whereabouts.

He was cursing, and his brain was slipping in and out of gear. He hadn't even seen the approach of Cassie Gilkicker when the gun blasted from a dark and narrow building gap on his right.

Cassie yelled for Reed, but *he* was already doing the same for Athol Cade. He was into a falling run and, as he went to ground, the large bullet from a Sharps carbine, pounded the air inches above his head.

In his peripheral vision, Reed held the flash from the darkness as he rolled on to his stomach. In a last-ditch, agonized effort, he raised a gun and fired, dragged at the action and fired again.

'That's it, Cade,' he said, dropping his head to the ground. 'Now I get to see you die.'

A group of people were now holding lanterns on the boardwalk. The light shone thin across the street, lit up Elias Claye as he stood unmoving in the gloomy gap.

Both of Reed's bullets had hit him. One in his chest, the other high and to one side of his forehead. Bright blood ran down his face, and he closed an eye as he raised the carbine.

Reed pulled himself to his knees, managed to get himself a couple of feet nearer to Claye. 'I saved one bullet for when we get real close,' he huffed.

'Goddamn you, Sawyer. It was Hite I wanted. You just had to make it you,' the one-time rebel guerrilla drawled thickly.

'It could never have been any other way, you murderin' scum,' Reed rasped. 'You killed my family, an' I've waited five long years for this.' It was Reed's raw anger, his need to see retribution, that held off the sucking pit of blackness.

Cawden Fisher had pulled Cassie on to the boardwalk, where he was preventing her from running back into the street.

'Reed,' she pleaded. 'Reed, please, that's enough.'

'There's folk here who'll testify to murder. You'll hang for it, Sawyer,' Claye choked.

'I got to kill you. I promised my sister. An', oh yeah, I promised Packman, too.'

Claye responded to the taunt from Reed. 'You ain't killed me yet, you son-of-a-bitch.' With that, he lowered the barrel of his carbine down towards Reed, shuffled a half-step forward.

'We can send him to Santa Fe. They can put him on trial there,' Cassie was still insisting.

But Reed wasn't for swaying. To his way of thinking, there was no need. He dragged himself upright, his breathing quick and shallow. With the exertion tearing at his lungs, he drew back the hammer of his Colt for the final shot. 'I guess *this* is goin' to have to be that other time I wanted, Captain Cade. Looks like you got your cockade back,' he uttered with quiet contempt.

Claye dropped his carbine and raised a hand to his sticky forehead. He took a fascinated look at his fingertips, made the death grin as his eyes clouded. He fell stiffly, his bloodied head thumping face down into the hard-packed dirt at Reed's feet. Reed was headed the same way, but he didn't quite make the full journey. Cawden Fisher caught him as he fell. Cassie Gilkicker picked up the Colts, let the hammer back against the bullet that wasn't needed.

22

THE TREATY

It was approaching first dark in Las Vegas. The light, peppery scent of bluebonnet lupins drifted through the open window of Catherine Gilkicker's small house on the edge of town.

'Where's my guns?' were the first words Reed uttered, on regaining consciousness.

'*Gun*,' his sister corrected. 'One of them's mine, remember?' Mina was sitting on the edge of Cassie's bed.

Reed's eyes took in the room. 'Back in the Sawyer Infirmary,' he said, tiredly, to Cassie. 'Could nurse maybe run to a cup o' tea?'

Cassie smiled warmly, shook her head. 'No. Doc said you're too full of painkiller. Anything else would make you sick, right now.'

'Yeah, I helped myself to a spoonful o' that happy juice. Sure takes the edge off whatever ails you.' Cawden Fisher said, from where he stood in the doorway.

'Hmmm. How's Mercy Claye?' Reed asked him. 'You look out for her, like I told you?'

'Yeah. Before one o' them Big Greasewood waddys took care o' her, it looked like.'

'Thanks, Cawden,' Reed said. 'Guess we'll all have to drop the "kid" bit from now on.'

Cassie nodded in agreement. 'We've been waiting for you to come to, Reed,' she said. 'We've all been talking and we've got something to put to you.'

Reed looked again at the faces around him, saw the anticipation. 'I hope it ain't got anythin' to do with land deeds. I don't think I could—'

'Well it has, and it hasn't,' Mina interrupted him.

'That's right,' Cassie agreed. 'You see, we think we're owed, all of us. But we can only get payback from the land. What's known as Big Greasewood.'

Reed closed his eyes for better concentration as Cassie continued, 'Mercy doesn't want to stay out there on her own. And now she sees herself as a squatter . . . accepts *my* claim as legal.'

Reed opened one eye. 'Why doesn't *she* fight you? After so many years, she must have rights.'

'She *does*, and she inherits them as well. But she doesn't want any more fighting, for goodness sake. None of us do.'

'How do me an' Mina figure in this?' Reed asked, going with his line of thought.

'We owe *you*. Owe you more than anything. This

is our way of repaying you both.'

'What way?'

'With an equal share in the land. A tenure with formalities . . . proper paperwork.'

For a moment, Reed considered the breadth of the proposition. 'A co-operative eh? You don't think that land's got some sort o' hex on it, then?' he suggested lightly.

Cassie shrugged. 'Mercy said you might think that. If it turns out, we'll find the Castanars. Sell it back to them. But I'm sure that's not going to happen.'

'If you're not interested, there's plenty of *other* work. The town's goin' to need a sheriff, *and* a proper undertaker, if *you're* still around,' Mina offered with a mixture of cheek and cheer.

Reed looked caringly at his sister. She'd been hurt in so many ways, and he was moved when he saw the hope and desire written across her face. He also saw the glances exchanged with Cawden Fisher.

'You sure that Mercy's agreeable to all o' this?' he asked of them all.

'Yes,' Cassie replied. 'It was *her* idea. Besides, she said she wants some new kin.'

'Well, in that case, it'll be real fittin',' Reed said, not entirely certain what was meant. Then he looked again at Mina. 'We'll build a fine cabin. You know, walls an' all.'

'Maybe one day. We'll need good money for that,' she replied wistfully.

'I got it, sis. A plump, gold poke. A feller up near

Winding Chair Ridge owed us. You remember?'

While Mina was thinking back, Reed asked about Mercy. He was suddenly concerned by her absence, almost surprised by the fact that he wanted to see her.

'She's gone to Albuquerque to get that proper paperwork drawn up,' Mina told him with a knowing and cheerful smile.